SURVIVING
SERIAL LOVE

SURVIVING
SERIAL LOVE

PAM HOVLAND & EMILY HOVLAND

CITI OF BOOKS

CITIOFBOOKS, INC.
3736 Eubank NE Suite A1
Albuquerque, NM 87111-3579
www.citiofbooks.com
Hotline: 1 (877) 389-2759
Fax: 1 (505) 930-7244

Ordering Information:
Quantity sales. Special discounts are available on quantity purchases by corporations, associations, and others. For details, contact the publisher at the address above.

Printed in the United States of America.

ISBN-13:   Softcover   979-8-89391-808-3
                    eBook   979-8-89391-809-0

Library of Congress Control Number: 2025914485

~SURVIVING SERIAL LOVE~

S he grew up in a small town. So small, everyone knew everyone's parents, grandparents, aunts, uncles, cousins, nieces and nephews. When people moved away for jobs, or college or just to explore the rest of the world, when they came back to small town America, everyone knew them and their place in town and where they had been.

It was that kind of small. No crime other than maybe petty theft by some school kids. Maybe an auto accident occasionally for some excitement. Possibly a fire once every 10 years or so. Quiet. Safe. Neat. Clean. Lovely.

Her mother had remarried a man who was new in town. Her first husband, the only man she had children with, died unexpectedly in an accident nobody witnessed. It was a freak accident, but the autopsy results were inconclusive. It was ruled an accidental death and left at that.

As traumatic as his death was, it helped her pay off some bills, the mortgage and get her children set up with trust funds for their future. She was so busy trying to take care of her children's future, she hadn't stopped to consider this one man's face who kept appearing when she was nearly at the end of her ropes. He worked at the local bank and was extremely helpful with her many financial questions. She was so engrossed in her late husband's business and issues that needed tending to that she hadn't asked anything about him. She knew he had been in town for a year or so. That he apparently came here for a change of scenery from his late wife's death. He could no longer live in the house where they were a couple. He couldn't ride the horses they had ridden together. He could no longer sit on the front porch and watch the sunset without her.

So he found a very small town to move to where it was quiet. No crime. Everyone knew everyone and trusted each other so much, they never bothered to lock their doors or windows at night. People preferred to get as much of a cool breeze through their homes as possible. It just felt better when they woke up each morning to fresh, clean air, knowing it would get thick & heavy, harder to breathe during the day.

He was looking for that kind of small town. And he'd found it.

When she finally realized how much he had been there for her, patiently answering or researching each and every question she had no matter how insignificant it seemed. She found herself considering how attractive he was. Beautiful, gentle, soft blue eyes. Not really rugged good looks but definitely manly good looks. Strong jaw. Nice lips. Clean shaven. He'd look great with some facial hair, she thought. He'd look good in anything, she surprised herself! Or maybe nothing at all! Oh my! Now she really surprised herself!

She decided to come up with another insignificant question for this new mystery man at the bank, and to get all dressed up, try to look happy and healthy, smell great, and just smile as much as she could. Then she laughed at her own boldness, not thinking she could ever pull it off.

The next thing she knew, she was talking to him on the phone and setting up an appointment to meet and discuss her insignificant question. Like what's your name? Are you seeing anyone? Do you want to see someone? Like me?

She giggled, poured herself a glass of wine and headed to a bubble bath to ponder this new attitude that seemed to be taking over. She liked it. It had been a long time since her husband died. It was still sad, and lonely, but she was getting over it. And it felt much better than crying all day and night over something she couldn't change.

She hoped God and her ex-husband would forgive her if she was doing anything wrong, but seriously, at this stage, it felt like progress, moving on, rather than some sort of sin. And she was so ready to begin laughing again. To feel pretty. Wanted. To flirt and feel like a woman again. A living, breathing, passionate woman. And it made her feel giddy.

Even her children seemed to appreciate new attitude. They had been broken hearted when they got the news about their father. He was a good man. A great father. He had so much to teach them. She always got to sad thinking of what was taken from her children. And herself.

But hey! She has a glass of wine and a hot bubble bath going on right now, and the hope, finally, of a future in the fickle, sometimes impossible world of love.

The home and their lives took on a much happier attitude. There was singing and music in the house once again. She used to sing with her husband, and she didn't even notice that she'd stopped playing music and singing since she buried him. The music made life so much easier to face.

She still missed him each morning while drinking her morning coffee. That was "their time". The time they could calmly lay out their plans, thoughts, ideas for the day, and the near future, and know where things were going. It was their strategy meeting on their lives, their family. Now it was quiet. Somber. Even the coffee tasted a bit bland. But she bought herself some fancy new coffee, a new coffee creamer, a few other things to mix into her wonderful coffee and she put a small radio in the breakfast nook. Each morning she had better than Starbuck's coffee and beautiful music to start her day. She had obviously turned a corner and it suited her well.

She didn't tell her children immediately, not being sure how they would feel about it. As well, it effectively eliminated the incessant teasing that would go along with letting her children know she was interested in someone.

So once the kids left for school, work, friends houses, she began getting ready for her "meeting".

She took extra time with everything. It had been decades since she'd felt like this! She spoiled herself every step of the way, enjoying the process as much as she hoped to enjoy the result.

It was finally time to go. She hesitated, and then walked into the kitchen, the radio still playing happy music in the background, reached up into a tall cupboard, with the aid of the step stool, grabbed the tall necked bottle and poured herself a shot of whiskey. Just for courage, she told herself.

It still burned like hell going down. Just like she'd remembered. Maybe worse than she'd remembered. Anyway, she hoped it would give her enough courage to actually go through with her plan!

It was obvious "New Guy" noticed! His face brightened up when he saw her! He stuttered over his words. He pulled the chair out too far and it nearly fell over backwards. He grabbed his tie, actually bowed down in front of her and offered her the wayward chair, fully upright and sturdy for now.

She could not have been more pleased with her results. It was adorable! Her confidence soared! Maybe she didn't even need that shot after all! She was a hottie all on her own!

And it worked! After she had her insignificant question fully answered in several ways, he finally asked if he could call her sometime? He hoped it wasn't too soon, but that he'd been struck with her beauty the first time he saw her a year or so ago, but out of respect for her marriage, he kept it to himself. But, he explained, she looked so beautiful today, glowing maybe even, that he couldn't keep it inside any longer.

Of course, she said "Yes."

And then on the way home, she slammed on her breaks and gasped! She was so focused on looking wonderful and the resulting hoped for reaction that she didn't think ahead to the part where she must tell her children. And they are going to be relentless in the teasing.

And they were. He called. She whispered into the phone. She giggled. She ignored them. She was walking around the house, picking at nothing, and chatting on the phone. And then the kids looked at each other and started questioning each other. Is she talking to a MAN? Who could it be? They knew most of the men in town were already married. A couple of them were available but they just didn't really seem husband material. They didn't even seem dating material. Everyone in town would know they were just taking her out to make her feel better. Maybe score if she's drunk enough. A roll of the dice. But she couldn't see herself being married to any other man but her past husband.

Until Mr. Bank Executive came along.

"Who was that, Mom?" And "Who were you talking to all giggly like a schoolgirl?" Plus, "You don't have a boyfriend do you Mom? Mom??"

But she decided to immerse herself in the grooming process, the getting ready process. She was liking spoiling herself a bit. Her kids were nearly grown. They had outside interests. They left her alone often. It was the natural way of life. We as Moms, spend our children's' lives teaching them how to leave us. How to survive on their own without us. Roots & Wings it's called. We are to provide our children with roots and wings both. And make sure they know they are firmly loved along the way.

This home and her heart were the kids roots. And they were already fairly adept at using their wings. So, she didn't feel guilty about doing something for herself. Life had thrown her a huge curveball, but she had dealt with it and was successfully moving on. She felt like she could fly if she jumped off the front porch! Or opened the bathroom window and just took flight.

She chose to continue getting ready for her big night out after so many years, and ignore the silly comments her children made. They will be fine, she thought.

The evening was so perfect! He paid for her limousine. It picked her up at her front door and deposited her in front of the restaurant. As she walked in and explained whom she was looking for, she was escorted directly to his table. He saw her a split second before she saw him and he was standing up as she walked towards him. The maître d' pulled out her chair & she sat down. And noticed the two beautiful red roses in a lovely crystal vase on the table. He saw her looking at them and said they were hers. He bought them separately, asked permission to bring them in and place them on the table. So the roses didn't die, he bought the cut glass crystal vase as well.

She was so glad she took 3 long, leisurely hours getting ready. She felt worthy.

They ordered food and drinks but were told it would be a rather long wait. He asked if she would dance with him while they waited? As she listened to the music, she realized it was going to be a slow dance. Just what she needed. She hadn't danced in years either. She needed to start slowly! She felt like she was blushing as she said yes. He escorted her to the darkened dance floor, a hand on her lower back so she knew he was there. He smelled delicious. Just enough cologne that it didn't overwhelm the scent of his clothes, which also smelled great! His hair was awesome. She had already noticed his soft blue eyes. And she had plenty of dreams about his mouth. His hands. His other parts. 😌

After all she'd been through these past few years, she felt like life was going to be OK once again. In fact, she felt like she was in the middle of a dream rather than the nightmare she had just put away.

She was happy.

And this man was the reason. He gave her hope. He made her feel sexy as hell and deeply wanted. She could see herself in his arms. In his bed. In her life. But it was only one date! What if he didn't like her really and didn't ask for a second date? What was she thinking? She was getting way ahead of herself. It was probably because she felt so good finally after depression being her best friend for so long, that she was just letting her mind go with good feelings. She decided to let her mind wander all it wanted, knowing full well it was all just a dream.

She needed this.

And he seemed to say everything just right! He seemed to know her heart. Her soul. Deep inside her mind. It was as if he knew what she dreamed of since a child, and he talked about making it real. How on earth did he do that? Had she told him these things in all of the meetings before? Did she mindlessly babble on and on about nothing during the dark time that she was trying to deal with her husband's final issues? Did he remember every conversation, no matter how inane, and she didn't remember any of them? How did he know her so well already?

Their dinners came and she was able to gaze upon the lovely red roses and that beautiful cut crystal vase! They had sipped a drink between dances, had wine with dinner, a dessert wine with dessert and a nightcap! She was feeling wonderful! Well fed. Adored. Respected. Cared for.

She leaned back, rubbed her stomach and actually said, "I could get used to this!" And immediately regretted it! She was moving too fast! Too forward! Too much! She needed to dial it down a few notches! Chill.

"Me too." He smiled, rubbed his belly and looked at her to let her know she wasn't being forward. It really was a very nice evening. And that evening was probably exactly what most people would wish for at least once in their lifetimes! Several times per week would be pretty darn cool. Every night would be ideal! Haha!

To which he replied, "I could do this every night!"

See? How did he do that? Was he clairvoyant? At least an empath? How did he know her like a book already? She really needs to keep her mouth shut around strangers. Grief kind of takes the logic out of you. She made a pact with herself to at least take stock of her audience in the future.

But for now, she felt too good to consider anything negative. Just for tonight. She'd been living in a negative life for long enough! It was time to feel good about herself again. Her life. Her children. She felt like she was being a good Mom by taking a bit of time for herself to recharge. Get her thinking out of a rut. To think about something other than being a widow.

She felt free for the first time in so long and she really liked it! Emotionally, she was soaring. And she knew to keep a rein on it, but she also knew it was fun to let it fly for just a bit. Keep it on an elastic tether. Like a resistance band. Let it go as far as it wants, until it gets to the end, then reel it back in!

Just for tonight, and just for now she will allow herself to be happy. And then she'll go back to her quiet, mundane, boring life of a good girl turned widow. With children to finish raising. By the time they are all comfortable enough to leave home, she would no doubt be too old and tired to care. And nobody would want her by then anyway. Old, used up. Can't care for herself, let alone someone else. Who wants that in a woman?

This man had erased what could have become an even uglier life than the one she had been living.

But it didn't end that night. It continued on. And on. They didn't go to that expensive restaurant every night, but once a month they did. For old time's sake. He came over almost every evening after he had put the bank to bed. The kids were getting used to him being around and no longer teased their Mom when she got all dolled up. They realized how much she had been grieving for their dad and decided they liked her Diva lifestyle much better than when she was moping around, sighing, crying, blowing her nose. Didn't shower. Always in her worn out robe because their dad had bought it for her when they first married. It was nearly transparent by now, it was so worn.

Seeing her in a dress, or slacks, or even Levi's when she went to bon fire parties and being happy was just what her kids needed as well. They saw that it's ok to let her go and continue on with their own lives. They realized that this newfound friendship replaced so much that was missing in her life, and they realized it meant they had their own personal freedom back now as well. It was just an ideal life after so much sorrow.

She dearly loves her children, of course. Totally and completely loves being a Mom. But before she was a Mom, she was a woman. And that woman had been missing in action for far too long.

Things were running so smoothly now. There was talk about him moving in with the entire family. Since the kids were getting older, their focus was more on which colleges they could get into or where.? What's the coolest college party town? So when, at the family meeting where Trevor, Mom's new beau, was in attendance, nobody really objected to the idea of him moving in. He was here most every night for dinner anyway. It was all Mom talked about all day. It would be great for her to have someone to hangout with, go places, do things, talk to.

And so, he did. He bought each person in the family a special gift when he moved in. A gift that proved he listened to them, their hopes, dreams, questions. And expensive. When even the kids noticed it seemed a bit spendy, he made a joke about the bank actually paying for it, so enjoy! Everyone laughed and went on their ways.

They began having a drink together out on the patio while the sun sat. Just like when dad was alive. It was nice to hear her laugh again. The familiar tinkle of the crystal pitcher of drinks they decided to make up that evening. He BBQ'd a lot as well. The Grill~Meister. She even had a manly cook's apron made for him with that name.

It was very sweet, but a little gross to the kids. Every so often they would hear a sound come from Mom's room that they didn't usually hear. The kids would giggle and then go outside and play ball just for a distraction.

The only odd or unusual thing was the old childhood friend that kept hanging around with Trevor. Of course, he was her age now, an adult, but why would they have anything in common? They seemed to have completely different personalities. But as soon as her old childhood friend showed up, they took off to the garage, or a drive, or for a walk down the long driveway together. Childhood friend barely said hello. He never asked how she was doing. Never asked about her family, of which he grew up with as well. And there still seemed to be something odd about him. He hadn't grown out of it after puberty. If anything, he seemed even more odd. Odder? Trevor explained that the guy was lonely. Had trouble finding women. Wasn't sure even if he was gay or not. So Trev Buddy was supposed to be helping him "find himself" sexually. Which should set off bells and whistles alone, right? Maybe?

But she had enough negative in life the past few years. Feeling good felt so good she wanted to keep it going. Besides, it was his friendship, not hers. She didn't have to have anything to do with the old childhood chum.

In fact, she decides it's time for a party of some sort. It can't be an adult party because the kids will hate it. It can't be an all-kid party because the grownups will hate it. So, they make it a sleep over.

The children were encouraged to make their own decisions. They could go to a friend's house that night or they could have friends over. Four friends per person to sleep over. The 2 boys opted to go to a friend's house. Their dad was the local coach in town and was well liked by the townsfolk. For them, it would be a night of playing sports, talking sports, watching sports on TV. It would be an awesome evening for a young man.

So her daughter began making a list. She was hoping that now the boys were not participating, she could invite what would have been their friends and invite 12 girls over! Her Mom said no way of course! A houseful of 13 yelling, screaming young ladies was far more than she had signed on for! They argued and strategized back and forth. Yes, OK, then No, just 4 and then a compromise number but then they would disagree.

Her daughter finally relented, and they stayed with the original plan. She would be seeing most of her friends in college anyway.

The night of the sleepover, her daughter had noticed a certain shiny object on her mother's hand. She was so busy that her hands pretty much flew past her, like busy little birds flitting around, getting things done. And then a brief second that her mother's hands were still and there it was. A lovely but understated gold and diamond ring on her ring finger!

"Mom! Are you & Trevor engaged? Is that a ring I see on your completely capable hands?" To which Mom demurely replied that she & Trevor were actually married!

There was no mistaking the flash of deep hurt that resonated on her daughter's face. Why didn't you tell me? Why didn't you invite me? Why wasn't I your Maid of Honor? But she was speechless. But her mother knew these questions would come anyway. She explained that it just seemed they were so busy with their own lives, their own future plans, that planning a 2nd wedding at a courthouse seemed to be a rather boring event. And they both wanted to keep it quiet. Looking back, she could have made a big deal out of it. The entire town needed a reason to party, to celebrate! She could have held it in the park and invite the town. But she was a rather quiet, private person and preferred life that way.

Mother and daughter made plans to sit and talk about it later but for tonight, it was all about her sleepover. She chose her favorite friends that wouldn't, for some reason, be going off to college where she was. They picked other colleges, other towns, or just stayed around town, working, raising babies and continuing on. They were such a mangled group! One girl's family had more money than should be legal in her tiny town. One girl's family had a big, lovely ranch full of beautiful horses out below the foothills. One girl lived in town with her parents and one girl lived in town with a foster family. So they ranged from the privileged to the ones who could use some help from the privileged. But that never happened. You don't get rich by giving money away! And, watch your pennies and the dollars will take care of themselves! And the rich get richer and the poor still go hungry. In this little town, however, everyone got along as far as class went. Everyone seemed to understand their "place" in the little town. It was comfortable. Cozy. Secure. Reliable.

Trevor was out on the patio grilling hamburgers and hot dogs. He and Mom were taking turns mixing their drinks, talking, laughing, giggling, whispering to each other. Her daughter felt free to do what she wanted in the house since Mom was happily preoccupied. It kind of took the sting of not being told about her Mom's wedding off of her heart. A little bit. The gold on her Mom's ring finger flashed before her eyes. Nope. It still hurt some.

But she had guests, and topics to discuss. Coming home from college plans to make! They agreed to all meet at the ranch at the foothills and take a picnic lunch, all 5 of them, and meet at a meadow near the creek and waterfall. It was far enough away and up enough of a mountain that they would take the horses and make a full day of it. Horses, chatting, catching up, swimming, diving, eating great food and maybe even sneak in some alcohol! They all giggled at the thought!

And then it was time for dinner! The girls claimed they were famished. They came running down the stairs laughing, giggling, talking all over! They admired the table loaded with food a teenager would love but only Mom and Stepdad had the alcohol. The girls excitedly told her Mom all about their various plans. They were all so excited with the possibility of the future! Hope for an exciting life all on their own! No siblings, no nosey parents, no even nosier aunts, uncles or cousins!

Mom & stepdad watched quietly with smiles on their faces. The girls' excitement was contagious. Mom was thrilled to hear how happy her daughter would be without her. She would be able to live her life on her own and not still be connected by an umbilical cord. She looked at her ring that was sparkling even in the dim light of the outside porch and smiled to herself. She'll be fine, and so will I. She thought of the first dinner they had together. The limo, the food, the magic, and she was thrilled with the way her life, and her children's lives, were going.

After cleaning up, the girls went back upstairs to do whatever teenaged girls do when they're all together and their parents are distracted. Probably call boys. Mom & stepdad took a tray of chilled drinks up to their room. The night was extremely pleasant, and Mom was finally happy. Her heart relaxed. Her soul felt at peace. Her muscles actually seemed to say "Aaahhhh…" for maybe the first time in her adult life.

She was happy and it was totally unexpected.

It was so peaceful. It was perfect.

And then all hell broke loose, and it centered right in the middle of her house.

Her daughter came blasting into her bedroom bright and early the next morning. She thought a gun had gone off the sound of the bedroom door busting open and then almost immediately hitting the bedroom wall.

She sat bolt upright, mouth open, eyes wide and before she could form a thought as to what was going on, her daughter began to scream, "Andrea's gone! She's gone! Her stuff is here but she's gone! Nobody can remember the last time they talked to her!! Mom! Get up! Call the police! You gotta help! Mom!"

She hopped out of bed and ran to her daughter. She had to get some sanity into this situation to best pass on info to the police, but also to make some sort of order out of her home so that she could think of the best, quickest most logical next step. Call the police definitely, but also there needs to be a thread, a path. What happened to her, when and where? What time.

It may have seemed silly, but she made everyone hot chocolate with tiny marshmellows. Tiny colorful marshmallows. It got everyone to calm down, feel a bit safer. Now she could try and make some sense out of what happened? First, where have you searched? What have you done so far that lead you to believe she is gone? Why do you feel she's missing? Whom have you called to double check? Did she go back home for something quickly? Is her car outside? Did she sneak out to be with a boyfriend? Will she come walking into the door just as the police pull up? I mean, that would be fine, just embarrassing. But I'd rather be embarrassed that to have to ID a body. Especially of a friend or family member.

The girls explained that one of them had gotten up early to make coffee and tea. She didn't know hot cocoa was an option. She was drawn to the huge cluster of fresh mint growing in the bowl by the window. Mint tea for everyone! Now they were sharing mint in the hot chocolate while going over the disappearance of one of the guests.

Her car is here. All of her belongings; phone, purse, shoes are all still here. She has a boyfriend but he's out of town this weekend with his family, which is why she wanted to be part of the sleepover. She didn't want to be alone this weekend.

Did she have a premonition? Has she been harassed or threatened recently? Has she pissed anyone off lately? We quadruple checked her sleeping bag & the area around it, for a note. Any sort of sign as to why she wasn't in it this morning like she should have been. We looked all around her car, fully aware that we may be destroying a possible crime scene, but she didn't take her car. It may hold a note or a reason, but nobody took her away in her car. It will probably only have her prints all over it. It wasn't moved since she arrived the evening before.

The evening before. She let her mind wander over the girl's arrival the night before. She never mentioned having to meet up with anyone. She didn't request a wake-up call for any reason. She didn't mention anyone else's name during the evening that was requesting her time. We went through her purse and all the papers in her car. There were a couple of receipts on the passenger floor, but the items listed had been brought into the house. The party treats were still on the kitchen counter right this minute in fact.

They had called her parents and asked if they knew how to get into their daughter's cell phone. The parents offered to come over and help brainstorm to try and figure out if the girl was being unusually irresponsible or if there were seriously a police issue at hand. They would bounce ideas off their brains with each other, trying desperately to find a reason why their regularly responsible daughter would act so irresponsibly. Not only to give the police the best option for finding her, but also because the other possibility was just too much to consider. Not now. Not her. Not this child! Please don't make me face that level of heartache. Please God. It was on their minds the entire way. They had so much going on mentally they didn't quite remember the drive over. It didn't matter. They were there and the police had just arrived as well. They introduced themselves to the police and were all escorted into the house.

Coffee, pastries, and hot cocoa were on the table. A list of reasons why she left involuntarily on the table, and it was surrounded by all the girls. As the police and the parents settled into the chairs the girls mostly vacated. After everyone had coffee, pastry, whatever they wished, they all seemed to take a deep breath and then begin. They repeated the moment they all woke up and realized she was gone for what seemed the hundredth time, but it needed to be done. This was the official version. This report would determine if the police thought foul play was involved or if the girls had maybe best not watch scary movies late at night at sleep overs! After the police went through the evidence, took photos, made phone calls, ran background checks, ran vehicle plates, they requested everyone leave the house as it was, spend the day at the beach, or a hotel. Please leave everything as original as you can and find a place to hang out for the rest of the day.

And now it was real. The police think a crime has been committed against their daughter's friend. What do they do now? Where do they go? How can they help her? Do they just go back home, wring their hands together and worry? Did they give the officers enough information? Do they understand she's a good girl? She wouldn't sneak out to meet anyone. She was very upfront and honest about her friends and relationships. She was incredibly close to her family, especially her parents, and would not be so inconsiderate as to just disappear and make them worry like this.

After the police left, Mom offered to put alcohol in any of the drinks that wanted it. It was too much to take in and now that it was "official", that a crime had happened here and they had to leave, that their house was now deemed a crime scene, she needed a drink to gather strength for the long haul. She had hoped it would all have been a false alarm, but it isn't. A girl was abducted right from her very town, her home in fact. Her living room.

How responsible was she? And for what? To whom? She definitely didn't want to have to go through the loss of a child, so she definitely wouldn't have been the cause of it. But what happened? How did someone come into her house, and only that one someone, take a child and leave? Nobody heard a thing. No violence? No yelling, screaming? Kicking things over?

How could this have happened here? Right here? Last night? They were both in bed all night, sleeping after a bit too much wine and a lot of too much laughter. It had been an incredible night with him. Pushing, or touching, all the right buttons! She did wake groggily once or twice during the night. She remembers rolling over, pressing her chest against him and realizing he was a bit cool to the touch. She did remember waking once and sleepily, using only one eye with hair cascading down in front of it, seeing him walking naked into the bathroom. The light was already on, and it silhouetted his muscular body. She immediately fell back into a deep, satisfied slumber remembering the things that body had done to her body. She was so happily in love.

And then she woke up.

As everyone left to go tend to their own business, she went into her daughter's room and sat with her on her bed. She knew she had to leave as quickly and as cleanly as possible to save whatever evidence they could, but there must always be time for compassion with your own child. Mom held her weeping daughter, eyes red from crying. She tried to console her by telling her nothing was her fault and she needed to be strong to best help find her friend. Then they discussed which hotel they should stay at for the night. Or what attraction or movie they had wanted to see but never seemed to have time. They chose a hotel with the best restaurant and pool and called it good. It wasn't a reason to celebrate, but it was a reason for some much-needed distractions.

They let the police know where they were and that the house was now open if they were ready to begin their investigation. As that distasteful but necessary task was completed, they just sat and stared at each other, wondering how it went from blissful and beautiful to something so deeply disgusting? And in their own home! Not just in their little town where crime never happens, not just "in their lives", like hearing it about some distant acquaintance that lived across town. "Did you hear so and so was beaten last night?"

But this was right from a sleeping bag, right in her very living room. She wasn't sure why, but she felt like throwing up.

Sympathy for her parents probably. Complete fear for the girl herself. Where is she? Is she OK? Is she safe and warm? Is she hungry? Why can't she get home? Is she scared?

Mom remembered something she'd forgotten. She called the police department & asked if she could drive back to her home and pick up her extra medicine. She didn't realize how low she was on it until she had a chance to sit and think. The police located the medication and said to drop by and someone would meet her there, in the street. She made a list of things she needed to pick up and so had a few places to stop before she returned. She asked if anyone needed anything and said that this was the last time tonight that she was going out, so if anyone needed anything, now was the time to speak up.

With her list in hand, she left the hotel room. She was so tempted to swing by the beautiful hotel bar and have a shot of tequila. A little bolstering for a difficult time. But she was going to go directly from here to talk with some police. Maybe she'd better not.

She got her meds, looking at her home like it was a stranger. There were lights and tape all around. The lighting was just not right. She'd lived there so long, but it looked like a stranger's place. She shivered, rubbed her arms, and walked back to her car. She completed all of her errands and was on her way back to the hotel. This time she definitely was going to stop by the bar and have a drink before she went upstairs. In fact, while she was in the bar, she called and asked what everyone wanted for dinner and called it in while she was there. She was hoping that by the time she had finished her drink, dinner would be just about at her doorway when she got there. She was just too exhausted to make it up to her room, ask what everyone wanted, and then make the call. She'd be asleep by the time room service arrived.

So, she called in everyone's dinner order, gazed at the beautiful blue sparkling pool and slowly sipped her lovely, exotic drink. She was considering if there was enough time to take a dip in the pool after dinner perhaps? That would feel heavenly! To float, weightless, totally relaxed, for just a moment! She asked the bartender what time the pool closed, and he said it could stay open all night providing nobody swam by themselves. If you had a buddy with you while you swam, the pool was open.

She was estimating the prospects that her daughter would spot her tonight after dinner so she could take in a really nice, long, leisurely, definitely needed to recharge my batteries swim, and decided it would be 50/50. Everyone was in that kind of mood. Lackadaisical, but also afraid. Will they be back? Will they come for another girl? How did they know all of those girls would be there tonight? Was it a scorned boyfriend of one of the girls? Just trying to show them how much they needed the boys for protection when they were the ones doing the crime?

It was too much. She couldn't sit here any longer. A child was missing. A child was missing from her home! She finished off her drink and headed to the elevators. She wouldn't give her daughter an option. She just had to go swimming with her mother tonight. Her mother needed to go swimming.

They had an incredible dinner, wine, drinks were in the locked bar. It was lovely. On any other night, it would have been memorable.

Tonight, it was just a very lovely diversion, but also nutrition. It seemed like strength was going to be needed here and a hot, nutritional meal was one way to get/stay strong.

After dinner and drinks in front of the hotel room's fireplace, the lights of the city twinkling outside, it was a pretty magical moment. This feeling was much preferable to how her morning had started and she wanted to bring this type of feeling back to her life. She instructed her daughter to grab her phone and her favorite book or magazine and come with her to the hotel pool. She even promised her daughter a hot fudge sundae after the swim to further entice her. Mama needed a few moments to relax and recharge. She felt like she was in the Dust Bowl in the prairie and watching a giant hoodoo heading her way. No trees or mountains to deflect the vicious wind and the dirt that can find its way into the house, through the windows! Where does she put her Babies so they are safe and can breathe? Will her animals survive? Her garden? Was this impending doom going to totally destroy her way of life, or was there something she could do to buffer her livelihood and her Family?

Forcing herself to relax and renew, she shook her head to get the thoughts to fly away for now. She slowly swam over to her drink, took a long pull, enjoyed the coolness of the remaining ice cubes and prayed the alcohol would soon do its trick. She wanted to float on her back in the warm, therapeutic water and let the alcohol wash over her brain, her nerves, and let her just exist for a moment.

She checked on her daughter, received an irritated grunt for her reply and then dove gracefully back into the warm water. She swam around a bit, did a few underwater moves and even sat on the bottom of the pool for a minute. Then she swam to the surface and flipped over. She blew out the old air like a dolphin or a whale would and exhaled as much of the air from her lungs as she could. Then she took in a deep cleansing breath and held it in her lungs for the added buoyancy. She steadied herself quickly, so she felt comfortable on her back in the water and stared up at the night sky. She could actually see some stars! In spite of the big city lights, there were stars above. She began thinking of when she was a child and lived on a ranch. There were a few lights, but you could mostly just sit on the front deck and look up. The Milky Way! We were even far enough north that we often got the Aurora Borealis lights!

She found herself thinking of a time when she was much younger when her little truck broke down one night on the way home. She was almost within walking distance, but it was dark and cold, and she didn't have a cell phone then. As she has resigned herself to walking at least to the next house, a car passes her going in the opposite direction. She didn't think much of it because they kept going. But then she heard the car go around the corner and slow down. She perked up her hearing because it was unusual, what this person was doing. It may have been a concerned neighbor and she'd feel like a fool, but they'd laugh about it on the way to her house. As she's trying to think about which of her friends has a new car, she suddenly hears it basically sneaking up on her. Behind her back. She takes a step off the road to a safe place on the shoulder. She waves at the headlights, hoping it's someone she knows. But as the car pulls up next to her, she realizes she has no idea who this person is. She hasn't seen them before around here. She has no idea which family he may resemble because he doesn't resemble any families that she knows locally. But why would a complete stranger be driving in the woods so late at night? She shivers and explains that she just lives up around the corner and her dad and brother are on their way to pick her up. She said she flagged down a driver and asked them to call her family. They were in a hurry but agreed to call when they got to the local grocery store just down the road.

The fact that he didn't realize there was no local grocery store just down the road further solidified the fact that he didn't live nearby. It also hit home that she was totally alone, in the dark, still at least a mile from home with no way to call for help. The driver actually became a bit gruff and aggressive! It took her by surprise, and she stepped back a bit more from the car. He angrily put his car into gear and grumbling under his breath, took off and scattered gravel when he left. Obviously, it angered him that she wasn't going to get in his car. That really scared her. But she'd seen enough inside his car to see that there was no back seat, no passenger seat, and no door handle on the passenger side door! Plus, the fact that he turned around to offer her a ride. No time constraints. Nobody is expecting him. He has all the time in the world to do whatever he wanted to do.

Knowing he would no doubt be really mad because a female got over on him, once he realized there was no local store, he may well come back to show her a lesson. As he peeled out in his car, went to the next corner and turned around, and glared at her as he drove past, she knew she had to hide. How far would he go to find the local grocery store? A mile, two? Ten? Would he just keep going, all pissed off that he'd been lied to and come looking for her, knowing how vulnerable she seemed?

She decided to take a shortcut through the neighbor's place. It would no doubt slightly anger them that someone had bothered to knock on their door without calling first, but this was kind of important. There was a stranger in town getting mad because young women wouldn't get in his creepy car in the dark, on a quiet country road. They would forgive her. And she really didn't care if they didn't. She needed to get off this road and into a warm, safe, well-lit place.

Straight up the hillside she went. She was about a mile and a quarter if she walked along the road to her dirt road and then up that dirt road to her home. She knew if he came back, angry, and drove along that road and not see her, he would naturally drive down the dirt road looking for her. She wasn't going to be safe until she was inside a home. A home of someone she knew. She took the driveway up so as to not leave a trail in the brush. It was only about 30' farther than where she stood but it seemed the risk of time would be safer. Would he really drive up this driveway looking for her? Or the next one? Or both? So, she took the driveway until she could see the lights from the house and then she tore through the brush to get there. She shook as she knocked on the door as the realization of what was happening finally settled on her.

"Who is it and what do ya want? Why you here at night?" A gruff voice came from inside.

"It's Me! Someone tried to pick me up on the road and I need you to call police and my folks, please? And may I please come in? I don't want him to drive up here and see me! He might involve all of us in some sort of horrible plan! Please let me in? Or at least call police?"

The door opened quickly, and she was flooded by blessed light! And a blast of warmth!

"Come in! Warm up! Tell us what happened? Are you OK? Who was it? What did they look like?"

The wife was both holding the phone and a cup of tea. She was talking to the police while she handed the girl the cup of tea. After she talked to the police, she called the girl's mother and father. They basically just lived over the hill about a quarter mile away, but it was closer to two miles by car. Not sure how long it would take for them to get here. But they did! They burst in with all of the same questions the neighbors had pelted her with. And the same questions the police would pelt her with. She was getting tired. Exhausted really, from the sheer fright of her experience!

They lived on the outskirts of a very small town. Not too many strangers ever come this way. Hopefully the police will find him and take him in.

The police finally did arrive. They had looked for a stranger's car on the way to the neighbor's house. They didn't see anything. Nobody. They took her report, told them to call if they see anything suspicious and left. It honestly felt like they didn't believe her. She caught a few sideways glances from the neighbors as well. And maybe even her parents. She felt heartbroken. Why would she make up such a story? She was a very quiet person, didn't like the spotlight on her. She was uncomfortable with being the center of attention, so what would be the point of making up this story and then actually involving other people in it? There was a lot of head shaking and side eye glances, but nobody said much to her. What if they didn't believe her? Not only her reputation but what if he came back and she needed help? Would they actually help or just shake their heads? She stayed vigilant and kept an eye on her surroundings, but eventually her fears subsided, the police and neighbors found other things to be appalled by and it slowly dissolved into the small-town gossip archives.

A sound startled her out of her reverie. Her daughter was standing near the side of the pool, her book, drink and phone in hand and asking if she can go back to the room now. Mom realizes she's actually doing a bit better but also wonders why this flash of a memory chose to surface now? Why now? Nobody made a big deal of it. Nobody knew for sure what to think. She was an honest little person, well respected and trusted in her little town, but this story just didn't fit. We don't have strangers stealing young women in the dark of night in this tiny town. That's why we all live here. For the peace, quiet, safety. Where Family is the center of the universe. Other than kids stealing pieces of candy from the grocery store, there is no crime here. So why would a local make up a story that brings crime to your tiny town? People still didn't know what to think about the stranger driving around, so they didn't. He never showed up anywhere. Not in their town, not in any town nearby. Maybe she was dreaming. But her car was still out of gas. Explain that one? That was how her story began. How could it have become fiction later?

So, the townsfolk let it drop. They wanted to continue to respect the young girl, but they also didn't want to think that crimes like that could happen here. They chose to let it die.

Eventually, life returned to normal, and she began to relax. She was busy with her upcoming wedding to her high school sweetheart. It was a wonderful diversion, and it gave the townsfolk something to discuss with her other than the mysterious man driving around with a stripped-down car.

After the wedding ceremony, which saw the entire town invited, life became busy. They both had businesses to run separately, but now they had combined them. They were taking on each other's obligations so as to best work together and be more efficient. Her little brush with the police made her semi famous local person. People would order from her and her new husband sometimes just for an excuse to talk with her. Ask her questions. Did she ever find any answers?

Eventually those questions were replaced by her asking questions about raising babies. She had become pregnant and was the happiest she'd ever been in her life! Eventually that line of questioning dissolved into the annals of recent gossip. Her new life, new babies, new husband all took over her time, her thoughts, and her duties. She didn't think about that scary time ever again.

But she also never forgot.

The next thing she knows, she's planning her 20th wedding anniversary! How did that happen? It seemed just last week they got married. And the kids! They've gone from diapers to driver's licenses overnight! She loved her kids and was so proud of them.

She acknowledged her daughter's ever increasingly loud sighs and told her she'd be out of the pool is just a bit. She slowly swam over to the steps, taking in the feeling of buoyancy and lightness in every pore of her being. She willed the water to lighten and enlighten, every cell in her being. She had a feeling she was going to need every bit of help she could muster from both inside and outside forces. She felt confident that she had rested and encouraged her body enough to face whatever may be just ahead of her and her family, and her tiny town. She certainly hoped so.

She slowly walked up the pool steps towards her towel. She felt the gravity pull at her body with each step she took out of the water. It felt like she had cement shoes on. Like she'd pissed off the old time Mafioso and they were retaliating. But she hadn't done anything wrong.

She dried her hair, wrapped it in the towel, grabbed her drink and caught up with her daughter. She suggested they get a hot chocolate at the bar. It would be fun and extravagant and another distraction. Her daughter rolled her eyes but sat down. She was in a better mood. Her eyes were not as red or as swollen as this morning. She was actually quiet at times rather than crying and wailing. She felt her daughter was starting to handle things in a rational, logical manner so that she could discuss things with her, debate, ask questions, search for answers. Together. Like Family.

She couldn't resist and asked for a shot in her hot chocolate. She even asked if the barkeep would put a shot in her daughter's drink. Fortunately, she didn't look 18. And the barkeep, feeling something was amiss, didn't question the Mom. She thought that it would relax her daughter enough to have an adult conversation but all it did was make her giggly. She giggled about having to walk up to the room. She giggled over the concept of the elevator; a tiny room to take you to a room. She giggled over everything she could think of. It was both refreshing and unnerving. And when they arrived at the room, she walked in, sat on her bed, and fell asleep. Honestly, it had been a very long and especially horrible day. Getting through it had been almost a Herculean effort!

Even though she wanted to talk with her daughter, she was even more thrilled that her daughter had giggled a bunch before she fell asleep. She hoped she would have really great dreams to help get her past this horrific day.

As her Baby Girl slept, she made yet another drink for herself and her husband and sat next to him in the huge, overstuffed chair. He blindly cruised through the various channels with the remote while they began discussing the day's events. He had been unusually quiet. He was typically the man of the house. He handled and controlled everything. Not in a bad way, in a take charge so you don't have to way. She appreciated that in him. As much as she loved her first husband, he would allow her to make all of the decisions. She appreciated it, but she also resented it. She asked him for help in deciding things, but he just demurred to her choices. It hurt and irritated her, but he wasn't doing it for that reason. He was showing her respect and she knew that, but still, she wanted help with some decisions, and he just wouldn't.

So, she appreciated his taking charge. She still always knew that she both had final say and that she was free to say, think and feel whatever she felt, and it would be respected. She very much needed to bounce ideas off of somebody. This had never happened in her lifetime! She lived her life so it never would happen to her, or her family or anyone she knew. She needed help trying to figure out how to "file it" in her brain. How much was she responsible for? Could she have done something else? Did she handle everything OK? Did she tell the police all she knew? Did she tell them everything she could think of, so they didn't think she had any part of this? The faces of the young girl's parents flashed before her eyes. "Did I do enough?" She asked herself again. And again.

During this time, her new husband was there, but he wasn't. He was in the background. He was by her side usually, but he seemed more of an observer than a support system. Her children were obviously destressed, especially her daughter. But they all talked among themselves. Each one knew how the next one felt. They knew what each other was thinking. What they needed. He seemed more and more to just be "there". He didn't participate in the discussions, but he was there. He didn't speak to the police much, but he was there. He didn't tell her what he thought, but he was there.

She began thinking of the odd things he'd said. At first, she just chalked it up to not knowing each other so well and so she didn't get his sense of humor. Or she couldn't quite follow his train of thought. Sometimes she wasn't able to grasp even his ideas. When did that start happening? Understanding each other was one of the things that drew them together. She seemed to know her so well. Like he'd been studying her. Stalking her? And what was it he said about her first husband? That he seemed like a nice guy? When did they meet? And, now she had doubts. Really deep doubts. Like a huge, black abyss that she couldn't see the bottom of. Even if she tossed a rock in that hole, she wouldn't be able to hear it reach the bottom. And in her minds' eye, she didn't see him there beside her. He was more hiding in the dark, behind her.

And then she remembered a strange conversation she had with him. She was reminiscing about her first husband, some of the great and silly things he would do to make her laugh. He broke in and said, "Yeah, he seemed like a nice guy. But you know what happens to nice guys."

Her mouth gaped open, she could not either take in air or exhale. She just sat and stared at him at the callousness of this remark. Again, she had hoped it was because she didn't quite "get" his sense of humor, but there was nothing humorous about this issue. And when had they met? She was pretty sure he didn't move to town until after her husband died. Was he just being polite and agreeing that he was a wonderful guy, or had they actually met and spent time together?

But she had already unpacked a very full suitcase, both literally and figuratively, and she was exhausted. She would have to attack this later. For now, she just didn't want to be doing this by herself.

And what a horrible time to be alone. She was pretty grateful that he was there. She stopped by the girls' family every so often, taking food, sympathy, information & sometimes alcohol to their house. They appreciated the extra noise in the house. It became overwhelmingly quiet at times now. Late at night when one couldn't sleep, and the fireplace and overstuffed chair called your name. You just had to go. Read a little. Sip cocoa. Try to remember. Try to forget.

The hotel stay was just what she needed. She was able to recharge just a bit. Room service was exceptional. It was a bright spot in a very bleak day.

They returned to the home to find it a mess. The police had obviously gone through every possible spot in their home looking for clues. She tossed her bags on the floor, started some coffee, and began putting their lives back together. She cleaned for most of the day trying to scrub the memories of the night before away.

Her daughter ran to her room, slammed the door, and began crying. All normal there!

She and her brand-new husband began working together cleaning up the girls' messes, cleaning up the police's mess, cleaning up life's mess. Cleaning can be so healing, and the results are usually extremely welcome. Scrub, clean, put things where they belong. Then, after several hours of this, when you take a moment to sit down and have a cup of coffee, getting prepared for the next round, sometimes you look around and you've done it! You were so focused on cleaning and expelling the negative from your body, mind, abode and soul, that you didn't realize you had cleaned it all! No wonder you thought this would be a great time for a bit of a coffee break and see that it's all cleaned! You're done! Yeah! It makes the coffee taste a bit sweeter. It makes life a bit easier. It gives you hope that you can carry on. She sipped her coffee and smiled at her husband. She wondered if she would have been able to get through this without him. She was so grateful he was there for her. She reached for his hand and patted it as if to say, "Thank you for being here." And left it at that.

The next morning, she woke up and the sun was shining. A slight breeze was wisping through her open bedroom window. Her favorite sheer lace curtains billowed with the breeze. The sky was blue. She could hear the neighborhood noises; people talking, kids laughing, horns honking to acknowledge a neighborhood friend. Normal. Life outside was perfectly normal, and it was a stark contrast to the feelings swirling around in her home. A tornado of feelings seemed to be twirling free will in her home, in her life.

She stood up abruptly and said to no one in particular, "Well! It's time to get back to normal, isn't it?"

She tried to think of what she and her family would "normally" be doing on this day at this time. It was a Sunday morning, and they had the newspaper from the hotel. She thought she could find something to read in the paper to make her feel even more "normal" but there was so much hate, despair, politics, crime, stupidity. She couldn't read it. Time to go outside. Maybe garden a bit. She had some plants in one particular planter on her patio that needed attention. She grabbed another cup of coffee and this time, added a bit of whiskey to it. She even found herself wondering if she still had any weed in the house. And where was her pipe, even if she did find her hidden stash. There were matches in the kitchen, but she was pretty sure she could round up a lighter or two if she actually got serious about smoking some pot. And it was Sunday. A Sunday after a traumatic Friday night. She was still alive. Her family was alive and healthy, if a bit broken for now.

In fact, that sounded like a great idea. It would be a great little diversion to find everything she needed to get high and then she could get high. Sit on the patio, work on her plants and drink her coffee royale. She was pretty sure she'd be taking a nap later today! But for now, it seemed to be what she needed.

It was much easier to find all her paraphernalia than she had planned or hoped. In her extreme perfectionism and sense of responsibility, she had put everything together in a sock and put it lovingly and gently in a cigar box and placed it under her silky things in her top drawer. It was way in the back and even though she would see it peek through her clothing occasionally, actually smoking weed at her age seemed silly. It had been there for years. She took her little box and a smile downstairs to smoke outside on the patio. That shouldn't piss anyone off. She needed this.

She sat down next to her husband and showed him her cache like it was gold. She explained where she got everything, how long she'd had it and did he want to smoke with her? Did he want a coffee with a bit of whiskey in it? Did he want to just forget the last couple of days with her? To pretend they didn't happen. To recharge to best survive the tidal wave about to come her way.

But for now, she filled the pipe and gingerly lit it. She took a deep, cleansing pull on the pipe and held it deep in her lungs. Work your magic, marijuana! Make me forget these past few days. Cloud my brain so I can smile once again. Numb my body so I don't feel the pain. Please, just for a while, make me forget.

She felt her face smiling. Nothing she could do about it. She just had to smile, and it felt wonderful! She was glad she'd done this. Her home was clean, free of the police evidence hunting, they were gone, the sun was out, it was a beautiful Sunday morning and she wanted, needed, to feel good. She wanted her husband to feel this wonderful, so she handed him the pipe, which he declined. It kind of put a damper on her high but in all fairness, they had never discussed marijuana. She hadn't smoked it long before she met him, so it never came up. No reason. Until this very morning. She was very open about people's personal choices and totally against peer pressure, so when he declined, even though it hurt her a bit, she completely respected his opinion, his choice. She smiled at him, feeling love for him so deeply this moment, heightened, of course, by the pot. But he got up abruptly and turned away, walking into the house away from her. She should have followed him and asked what she had done wrong, but she didn't want to be wrong right now. She didn't want to baby someone else's feelings right now. Her children and her own feelings were all she could reasonably handle. He was a grown up. She expected him to handle his feelings and talk them over with her when they had the time.

What an odd reaction, she thought. Even though he may not agree with her thoughts, words or actions, he always nodded his approval in front of people, and then shared his opinion about the issue when they were alone. She really appreciated the respect. But this was an outright exclusion of what she needed to do to continue on. Surely, he could give her this much time. This much of a moment to be totally irresponsible and then recharge from it.

Rather than walk into the dark, cool house, she reached for her pipe and took another hit. And then a sip of her whiskey laced coffee. That should do it, she thought. Get me back to I don't give a piss about anything right now. She just needed a few irresponsible moments to best handle the rest of her life.

To her surprise, she began giggling. She found herself putting her new husband way on the back burner. Her children's feelings she would deal with when she sobered up. For now, she didn't even want to deal with her own feelings right now. They were too deep, too raw, too fresh.

But! She saw her plants and planters in disarray and decided they needed her help and attention. She began giggling again as she picked up her trimmers and began sprucing up her raised flower beds and their resident plants.

And it worked! She forgot, mostly, the past few days. She forgot the sheer terror on her daughter's face when she ran into her mother's room that morning. She was even able to forget she had a new husband who didn't smoke pot with her, not even on a very difficult occasion.

She worked, trimmed, replanted, sipped and puffed the first few hours of the morning. As she began to sweat, she looked up and realized how much time she had put in forgetting. She sat back and took stock of her work. Her flower beds looked beautiful again. They were neat, clean, organized. All the dead was trimmed away. Weeds pulled. Seedlings transplanted. It had to be getting close to noon. Back to reality now. Time to make lunch for everyone. She grabbed her coffee cup, now mysteriously empty, and her pipe, still burning a bit, and stood under the eaves in the shade to cool off and admire her work. She stood in the coolness and took a deep puff. She thought briefly that she would take a quick dip in the pool. She could imagine the sweet coolness envelope her entire body at once. How refreshing and invigorating! But then she giggled again and thought she would probably take a deep breath under the water and drown her darn self! Giggle, giggle! She remembered why she loved to smoke weed and totally forgot why she quit. Responsibilities probably. You can't be a loving, caring, responsible Mother and still smoke weed. Or drink. Or take prescription drugs and be a good Mom. So, society says! I might even be a better Mom on weed, ya never know!

She walked into her kitchen and placed her coffee cup in her clean sink. She was so happy that she'd spent so much time cleaning. She loved a clean home and this one was spotless and cozy again. She began thinking about where her children said they would be. She took mental inventory of where they were which allowed her to estimate what their states of minds would be. She felt confident each one was at a place that was warm, loving, affirmative. Her children needed positive energy and not just from her. They needed to know the town didn't blame them for the girl's disappearance. She had hoped they wouldn't avoid her and her children out of fear that someone would just vanish if they came to visit. Her children, while obviously deeply concerned, were going to be Ok. They were each hanging out with their most favorite friends, the ones where they call the parents Mom & Dad as well. She made daily phone calls mid-day to check in with the parents and get a gauge on how the kids are doing by the spare set of parents they had chosen when they chose their best friends. She felt good that they would all get past this, both as a family and individually. She was so proud of her kids at that point. They were strong, resilient but also loving and kind. She liked her children as much as she loved them. It seemed to be a bonus to actually like the people you've raised! Loving them is a given. Liking them as the people they have become is a crowning glory!

With her children cared for and safe, her home put back the way it should be, and now sparkling clean with no left-over crime residue, she grabbed two cups of coffee, no whiskey, and took them upstairs to be with her new husband. She wanted to snuggle as the pot made her more amorous, more sensual, more open to taking a moment out of her jam-packed day and just snuggle.

She made it carefully up the stairs without spilling too much coffee. She giggled as she opened the bedroom door with her foot and slowly walked into the room. She stopped when she saw the anger on his face. Oh dear! This is not what she had wanted to walk into. Try and lighten his mood and match yours!

Smiling, a bit overly cheerful to counteract his mood, she offered him a fresh cup of coffee. He asked if it had any booze in it and she said no. She thanked him for being patient with her while she fell from grace and smoked a bit of weed, drank a bit of booze, bright and early Sunday morning. But it wasn't every day that a child, a teenager, was abducted from her front room. To say she needed just a bit of a break was an understatement.

"Go take a shower! You stink like marijuana!" he growled at her! She had never seen him even a bit perturbed, let alone angry. This was a great new surprise, and she didn't like it at all. Just before she got to the bed to hand him his cup of coffee, she continued her momentum and walked back out the bedroom door, back down the stairs without spilling much coffee and down to the kitchen where she sat both cups down on the counter.

"What did you do to my coffee?" he growled again.

No, she thought, it doesn't fit. This isn't the sweet, gentle, caring man I married. The always positive, always, "We'll get through it together" attitude was one of the major things she appreciated about him and now, when she really needed him to support her, he became another huge negative in her life. How can I possibly deal with what's happened and his shitty attitude as well? It was too much. This is not what she wants in her family.

For a flash of a second, she regretted smoking any weed or drinking any alcohol. She was getting depressed again so decided to "sober up" by taking a hot shower, washing her hair, maybe a full-blown bubble bath with scented oils! Yes! That would both make her feel great but also help her sober up some so she could deal with this new turn of events, a spiteful new husband.

She reluctantly returned to her bedroom and gathered up the items she needed and took them to the downstairs bathroom. It wasn't quite as bright or luxurious as her own bathroom, but she really didn't want to be near her new husband. What a horrible turn of events. Not only has her daughter been extremely traumatized, her family and her town have been traumatized and he picks this time to let his inner demons show. He chose this moment, this time, to take off his mask and reveal his true self? To force her to admit that she had made a huge mistake and that it would take years to clean it up. She wondered about what kind of damage would be done to her children and her relationship with them after this sham of a marriage.

She knew she would have to break down at some point. She knew she had to cry her eyes out for all of the pain that was happening and going to happen before she could get her life back on track. But now was not the time. She had work to do. She needed clarity on her new marriage. If this was the real him and the caring, compassionate man she had fallen in love with didn't exist in this person. He swept her off her feet and right into his own personal dungeon.

Fuck it! Fuck it all! And as she began putting oils and bubbles in her steaming bath water, she dried her hands and took another huge toke off her little gold pipe. After a second, she giggled again and decided that she will fix everything wrong in her life and she could do it, but first, a very hot, very oily and scented bubble bath.

No alcohol this time. Apparently, she had a confrontation to deal with once she got out of her lovely bath.

But she didn't think about that. She focused on happy, positive, healthful things. She thought about her first husband and how loving and respectful her marriage was to him. She loved him so much. Still. She tried hard not to idolize him and make him out to be beyond a mere mortal, which he was, but he was truly a good man, and she did miss him terribly. Especially now. She knew he would be by her side, talking softly to her that they will get through it together. That he was right there, by her side, holding her heart in his hands and taking great care that it is not hurt again. And he never would have growled at her when she was at a low point in her life!

The differences between her husbands were now becoming glaringly pathetic. Her first husband wasn't a superhuman hero, but he was loyal, loving, faithful and kind. He would have been so gentle with her feelings right now. With the kids also! He would have conjured up a fun adventure to get everyone out of the house and into some laughter. And so, she would do that very thing! As she lay back in the steamy hot bath, she let her mind wander. Where had they been wanting to go? What new event or opening did they want to see? Any new movies out there? What could they do as a family to try and get back on track? How about a 4-hour horseback ride and picnic lunch at the ocean? They would ride horses through the forest and down into the sandy beaches where they could play on or off the horses. They would have a picnic lunch, play in the water and return in time for a BBQ, courtesy of the equine facility. It cost a lot, but then, what price can you put on sanity? Or family togetherness?

And then she just let her mind go and before too long, heard herself softly snoring but was too far gone to do anything about it. She gave herself totally into the calm and quiet and let herself nap in the bath.

She was completely startled awake when her husband opened the door without knocking or asking her permission to enter. "Passed out from the weed and booze I see?" and he walked back out of the bathroom slamming the door in disgust. What? Where did that come from? Who was this person? Last night he was the man she married; loving, compassionate, attentive, gentle. They had made incredible love, both slow and sweet and fast and passionate. He gazed lovingly into her eyes. He seemed to treasure the things she did to him and with him. She would hear him gasp every so often, so she knew she was having some sort of positive effects on him. But this angry, spiteful, and downright mean person! Who was this and what did he do with her husband?

Her husband. She realized she was thinking of him again. Her new husband was able to banish the hurt and pain from his death for a while, but now the hurt was back and with a new layer put on by her 2nd husband. She began thinking about the mysterious way he died. There were no witnesses, apparently. His car was found smashed into a tree just off the road he took to work every day. It wasn't a particularly bad or scary road and people were still wondering how a fatal accident could have happened where it did, as it did, when it did. No rain on the roads. No fog, snow, ice, sleet or black ice. It was a bright, beautiful summer morning that he was going to work. He had been especially sweet to her that morning. They woke up early together and spent some very valuable time just being together. Being best friends who also get to sleep together. She loved him so much! She thought about the first time they met, their first kiss, their first time, which was the first time for both of them. They had that. It was special to this couple alone. Maybe it was old fashioned, but it was a claim that they both appreciated and respected and treasured about their marriage. At that point, they were each other's first, and only.

And now she was doing things to another man that her husband had taught her. It seemed disrespectful to a degree, but it was all she knew about sex. And he didn't seem to mind one bit that she was a little limited on her lovemaking skills. She was open to advice and suggestions however, but he just smiled and said she was doing great! That she was an excellent lover and didn't need to change a thing. While she tried to delight in the feeling that her husband was pleased and satisfied with her limited lovemaking, it also seemed untrue. Condescending even. She felt like there was no way she could totally, completely satisfy him. She felt that he had some sort of fetish that he would pay a professional for, rather than risk losing her over some perversion. Was he into feet? Shoes? Bondage? Urine? She had read enough to know that there were some pretty disgusting perversions out there, but she didn't want anything to do with them.

By now, her high was gone, or waning, her bath was getting cool, and she knew she had to confront her new husband over his totally inproper and completely surprising change in personality. Apparently, she needed to clarify boundaries! She is allowed to do whatever she wants in her own home. It's been totally paid for by the demise of her husband, it was only her name on the title now, so that entitled her to be the boss of her own home. She wanted to know where that anger came from and how often it was going to rear its head?

She pulled the plug on the bath, stood up and grabbed the towel. She took the time to admire the way the oils made her skin almost sparkle. She still looked pretty darn good for an old Mom of 3 teens. She admired herself a bit in the mirror, brushed and fluffed her hair and wrapped herself up in her favorite silk robe.

She shook her head, cleared her brain, picked up her things and prepared to do battle.

She dropped some items off in the kitchen to be taken care of later. As she walked slowly back up the stairs where just over an hour ago, she had taken a cup of coffee to her husband, and it was rebuffed, she wondered if this attempt to define boundaries would be futile or if it would bring them a bit closer with the clarity of understanding.

She found herself knocking on her own bedroom door to test the attitude in the room. Knocking on her own bedroom door for permission to enter? She tried hard to swallow the anger. She didn't want to start a fight, but she wasn't going to be fearful in her own home. It had become her refuge and no amount of negative bullshit was going to change that for her. She told herself to stay calm, get her answers and adjust.

She heard a non-committal grunt from behind her bedroom door, so she gingerly tapped it open with her shoe, just as she had previously. He had a fresh cup of coffee. She only had her bathroom items and walked through and placed them back in her own bathroom. She thought about the fact he had run her off from her favorite soaking tub. He ran her off from her own bedroom. He was running her off from her marriage. It was time to talk.

She asked how he was feeling? Did he have any aches and pains that he wasn't expressing? Did he have a headache? Did he need any aspirin? Tylenol? Did he need his coffee heated up? When he said he was perfectly fine and what was this all leading up to, she explained how she felt being run off from her own bathroom. Where did his spite and anger come from? Was this the real him and the sweet, compassionate, caring man was a fake?

She explained that she wasn't passed out from the alcohol or the weed. She was emotionally exhausted and was relaxing in the bath when she fell asleep. And did he have a problem with her smoking weed in her own house? They had cocktails every night so she knew he didn't have a problem with alcohol or her manner of drinking it. It was just the weed, apparently.

Silent treatment.

She explained, a bit more forcefully, that she was trying to find the middle ground, the compromise of her amount of freedom he was going to allow in her own home. She further explained that she was going to do whatever she felt like doing and if he had a problem with it, he needed to express it now while she was trying to solve this issue.

Nothing. He wasn't even looking at her now.

She looked down at her beautiful, sparkling diamond wedding ring and almost cried. What had happened? Her happy, wonderful fairy tale wedding was now tarnished. She had made a mistake and she had to fix it.

"I think you should get a hotel for a few days." There. She said it. If this was how he was going to act, he needed to know it wasn't acceptable. He had to be put in time out for a bit. Think about what he's done, why and how to change it. Bottom line, his behavior was unacceptable, and it was her home and she needed to make a stand. As the pot and booze wore off, she became more confident. She stood her ground and told him she couldn't put up with that type of attitude at this time of her life. That if he couldn't be there for her, she needed to face it all alone.

She watched as he angrily pulled his old suitcase from the walk-in closet and began tossing items in it. She wasn't used to this type of behavior, this level of anger directed at her. And where did it come from? What had changed? He was calm with the police. He wasn't mad that they tossed the house looking for evidence. He was stoic.

Until now.

She wasn't going to witness her new husband behaving so badly so she left. He would probably stop tossing things and being so angry if she left the room. She walked back down her stairs, feeling like they were now tainted somehow, and walked into the kitchen. She tidied up a bit and grabbed herself a real glass. It was now past noon on a Sunday, and she needed a drink. Her daughter's friend was abducted from her front room, or so they think. And now she was testing the fact that her marriage was pretty much over. She had been used. Lied to. What was it he wanted from her? Why was he using her? What did he expect to gain from this marriage?

She heard him tromping down the stairs and rubbed the little pipe in her pocket. She reached up and ran her fingers down the drink glass. She expected him to say something mean and hurtful as he left, and she prepared for it. But he didn't. He didn't say a word. She was both glad and sad. Glad that she didn't have to deal with any more misplaced venom and sad that he had that attitude and had to leave. She realized she was witnessing the death of her marriage and she felt helpless to change the course of events.

One he shut the door, without slamming it, which surprised her, she grabbed her little pipe and took a long, deep hit. She had stuff to figure out and she was going to need some creativity to get it done. She also wanted to be able to just forget the past few days and the smoke would help her do that.

As she slowly exhaled her smoke up in the air, she watched it swirl and move with the airflow. Pretty little smoke swirls, circles, lines. It's nothing like the hurricane that seemed to be forming in her personal life. She appreciated the slow sensuous movements of the smoke. It calmed her somehow. And when she heard his car door open and the engine come to life, she smiled and took a deep drink of her champagne. As sad as she was that her marriage was a huge mistake, she also knew a brand-new beginning was about to happen in some manner and she wanted to celebrate it. Even if it meant the death of her marriage, she was going to celebrate the change. It meant she could spend this most precious time with her children before they moved away and into adulthood where they would be too busy for her.

And that seemed to do the trick! She was actually happy about not having to deal with such a negative and selfish person. She focused on the time she could spend uninterrupted time with her kids. She vowed to make this time special for them. Just them. She had already put her 2nd husband in the past.

Several days later the rumor mill began grinding away. She had been hearing stories about another teenager that had been abducted from a neighboring town. There were no hotels in her town and her 2nd husband wanted to hide from the press basically, so a local B&B wouldn't work. He didn't want to have to answer questions. He didn't want to be noticed. He chose a large hotel with a chain of other similar ones all across the country. He saw a cell phone flash once in a while, but no press cameras.

He checked in, told the front desk he's not expecting anyone and not taking any calls, and off to his room he went.

And then she heard through the rumor grapevine about the other teen. It appeared the police had a serial killer on their hands. Or at least a serial kidnapper. Teennapper. They hadn't found any bodies. Maybe he was just collecting them like that one guy with the 3 young ladies he held captive for 10 years or so? Maybe he had a spare room hidden in his house, from his wife and his family where he kept and tortured the young girls he took. Maybe they will be found alive.

With a heart full of hope, she began to pray, to talk with God. She gave Him this problem in her life because she knew it was far too big for her alone. She asked Him why and then gave Him her pain.

She knew it would all turn out OK, it was just going to be extremely painful until then. But as long as she had her Babies, she would be able to survive anything. Her Babies. She called each one and told them that their stepfather had been banished from the home for a few days and would they like to come back home and talk? She missed them so much since this new guy had appeared in her life and she hoped they understood how lonely she was. Maybe one day they would comprehend that once you've been in a very long-term relationship, like her 20+ years with their father, that it was extremely difficult to learn to live totally and completely alone. She hoped they would forgive her for making such a huge and stupid mistake at this point of their lives. She could be so sad about all of this, and she started to droop emotionally. She thought she might have to go shower now, after that lovely, leisurely, and oily bath, and have a good cry. But she didn't want to cry. She wanted to laugh! To dance! To be grateful that her children are all alive and well and healthy. She had been intensely sad recently and knew that if her husband didn't change, she was going to be sad for a bit longer, but that it would all work out. She had hoped to make it as easy as possible to get this person out of their lives and back to normal and loving and kind.

And then the front door burst open and her son and several of his friends came in, sounding like a parade! They headed right for the kitchen and the fully stocked fridge!

"Man! I've missed this fridge, Mom!" her son exclaimed as he handed out goodies to his friends. And it was then that she realized that her husband had definitely put a time limit on the fridge. He controlled their freedom to raid the refrigerator, like all teenagers do. He had implemented that they had to ask permission to get into the kitchen after dinner. She thought it was so that she didn't wake up to a sink full of dishes after doing the dinner dishes. Now she saw it as a power play.

In what other ways was he controlling their freedom? The fact that the kids didn't want to spend time at home and was separating them from her came to mind. She felt so guilty. She was so ashamed that she had done this to her children. Her very reason for living. But it was so subtle. It happened so easily, so quietly. And on her watch, too. And she had gracefully stepped aside with a flourish and allowed him to do so. At least she wasn't giggling. She wasn't smoking any weed back then.

She realized she had missed her son's friends being here. She usually smiled as she shopped thinking of the growing teenage boys, appetites wrapped in skin, I heard them called, devouring the food she so lovingly bought for them. She knew all of her children's friends and their parents and their homes. As they found something to eat and settled in some place to eat it, she was able to visit with them, ask about their parents. Their siblings. She realized again how long it had been that her children hadn't felt comfortable enough in their own home to be here. When the other kids arrived, she would apologize.

And then the door opened again, and the other two kids came in, friends in tow. They had a really lovely pool and were one of the more popular homes to visit. All of her Babies were home, and their friends and she both loved and missed the sounds of them all hanging out together.

"Is it true?" one of the friends asked her.

"Is what true?" she asked back. "Is he really the kidnapper? Your new husband?"

And there it was. Something so sinister she couldn't even begin to wrap her brain around the idea, even though it had been nagging at the back of her thoughts. He couldn't be, right? He just has an odd way of dealing with stress, yeah? But now it was totally out there in the open. This is the gossip. The rumor. The story is that she is married to a man who kidnaps children. And then what does he do with them? They didn't have a basement, so no dungeon at this house. She was aware he had his own place before they met but it was a tiny little apartment above someone's old Victorian house. A screaming teenager would easily be heard. His car seemed clean. She had opened it up one day just to smell it. To see if it smelled even a tiny bit like the girl who had vanished. Unfortunately, it smelled like he had spent an awful lot of money having it meticulously detailed. It just smelled fresh and clean. Showroom clean. So why?

And she was appalled! "NO" her brain screamed! How could he be? He was in bed with her all night the night the girl disappeared. Maybe she went outside for some fresh air, and someone took her then. Why did the crime have to happen IN her home? In her very living room?

"No. He could not have done it." Was her flat reply.

But did she believe it? She turned her face to the sun and let it soak into her skin. She took in a deep breath of fresh air and filled her lungs, her soul with it. And then she grabbed her champagne and walked upstairs. Again, she felt herself, for the 3rd time that day, trudging up her Berber carpeted stairs, her feet feeling like cement, her heart even heavier.

She found herself wondering what if? He was the only person in their little town that nobody knew. Surely having worked in a bank, he had a complete background check done, right? Someone in town had to have checked with someone in his past and verified he was a good person, right? What did they know about him after all? That he was new in town. That his wife was deceased. Her husband was deceased. Oh, my gawd no. Don't even go there!

She decided it was too much for her to handle right now. She decided to hang out with the kids and find out what the rumor mill was churning out. She listened to their cases and turned each suspicion over in her head. Where was he at these times? How much can I defend him? Do I know where he was all of the time? And what about the girl that went missing in the same town that he had stayed for the time being? But it couldn't be. The kids are just jealous. Now that the grind and routine of a working and schooling family was in place, they were just envious that there was someone else in their mother's life. But they were leaving soon, and she would be alone.

Totally and completely alone.

And she didn't want to be alone. She had to admit, they had some pretty compelling stories. But it was too much for her to dissect right now.

"Ok, everyone! He's not a serial kidnapper and I'd appreciate it if you would find a different subject to destroy. How's the football team shaping up for this coming year? Anybody know?

Groans and moans came from the living room, patio, and pool. They wanted to discuss the crime. She let them run with it, providing they offered information they absolutely knew to be true. People have lost their lives to misinformation. Random speculation. Blame.

The kids hung around and ate, talked, laughed, and caught her up on their families. Eventually they began leaving, one or two at a time, to get ready for the night's activities. She was happy to have provided a great afternoon of food, family and fun before they all took off again on their separate lives. She asked her Babies if they would all come home that night, so she wasn't alone all by herself. They said they would and maybe even make a tent in her bedroom like old times. That made her entire day to hear that! She thought about which blankets she could use and if all of the flashlights had batteries so they could scare each other with ghost stories! She was so excited for the night!

After the last one had left, she changed into her bathing suit and went for a long, leisurely swim. She found herself, in the middle of trying to strengthen and heal, wondering if her 2nd husband could have kidnapped that girl.

No. She couldn't go there. Besides, the other girl was taken from a different town. Where her 2nd husband was currently residing. She shook her head to get those thoughts out of her brain. He might be a narcissist; it doesn't make him a killer. Or did it?

Too much! Too much to take in right now. Too much to deal with. She swam gracefully over to her champagne glass and took a few sips. She thought about her pipe but didn't want to get out of the warm water to go find it. So, she took another long sip of champagne and drank it down. She felt the instant relief as it went down her throat. It was cold and bubbly and offered numbness. Just what she needed right now.

It seemed as if a 3rd child would have to go missing before a definite pattern was set. Which town would it be from could be very telling. If it's a different town than the past 2, it would be a stranger on the move and on the prowl. It wouldn't be one of the stay-at-home town folk. It wouldn't be him. And it was sad that she had to think about another child being taken from their families, from everything they've known, and suffered a fate nobody knows about. But it would set the pattern and maybe make it obvious that her husband was not the serial kidnapper.

What a place to be in life! Wondering where the next child will be stolen from to prove the man you married isn't guilty? She totally hated him right now. She totally understood how her children felt about him now. She felt horrible once again. To distract herself, she would clean up the kitchen from its latest teenage invasion, make herself something to eat, grab her champagne bottle and go to her room. She needed a time out and she was going to use that time out time to get pleasantly drunk.

She awoke several hours later, and it was dark outside. Oh no! She had left the patio door wide open. The doors and windows were unlocked, and the lights were off. And there was a kidnapper on the loose. She got up and began her new nightly ritual. They hadn't had to worry about locking up at night before this happened. There was even a neighborhood dog that found its way into their house sometimes at night. It would be sitting in front of the fridge, slowly wagging its tail, begging for something to eat. And it was hugely overweight already but who could resist such an adorable sight? She would give the dog a good-sized piece of cheese and lead him back outside, firmly shutting the door behind him. Even then, she didn't think to lock it.

She completely shocked herself when her mind went to the thought that had she been locking her doors when she first was married for the second time, was she locking the serial killer INSIDE with her? And her children?

She felt so shocked by the idea, she had to stop, stand perfectly still and breathe as deeply as she possibly could to try to keep from panicking and also from fainting. How in the world could her loving, gentle, rational, nurturing brain come up with such an incredibly bizarre idea? It was so off the track of her usual every day thinking she had to stop. She dug deep in her brain, possibly way back to her childhood to question why she would think someone who loved her could also possibly harm her so deeply. And her Babies too. She never had flashbacks of her childhood. She didn't remember any whispered conversations among the adults in the gatherings. Nobody slipped and mentioned any previous abuse in her life. But then, her father did leave the family when she was very young. He was seldom mentioned again. It was her loving stepfather who had stepped in and lovingly raised her. He even adopted her, and she always considered him her dad. She never questioned it. So, maybe it was time for a conversation with her mom as well. She was raised to never be in fear. She was raised in a loving, trusting home so where this deep shiver of fear came from, she couldn't know. But she needed to.

As she was locking the patio door, she thought she saw him. Something moved in the bushes between the houses, and it was big. Not a cat or dog size. She tried to make it out, even calling his name, but nothing. She's just being paranoid right now, right?? He was in an entirely different town. It wasn't him. She finished locking up and went back upstairs. She thought about making herself dinner but grabbed the champagne bottle instead. She was surprised she hadn't drunk that much of it. There was still some left. She turned on a chick flick, poured more champagne into the beautiful glass and rubbed the pipe in her pocket. She was just going to enjoy this moment until all the Babies came back home. She'll probably need to make a run to the kitchen for some munchies before too long. Did she have brownie mix? Did she have enough weed to make magic brownies? What would her kids think? Could she call them and ask them to pick her up a bud or two? Did her kids even smoke weed? She didn't know. It hadn't been an issue in her family, so she never asked.

Eventually the gossip slowed down as people found other things to be judgmental and snippy about. They did at times treat her like a felon. Guilty by association, apparently. It was my new husband therefore I must approve of the kidnapping. So far from the truth. So cruel to make up such a story. But she lived here her entire life. Her parents still lived here. Her brother and his family. Her sister and her family. Her children needed a home, a nest, to return to. This one was just perfect for that. Until now.

She had tried so hard to distract herself from what had happened, but it seemed it was time to sit down and really try to understand what had happened and why. She hadn't talked to her husband for quite some time. She was beginning to wish he was here to help her. Comfort her. He wasn't the children's father, but he was a male presence. She needed a partner to deal with this. She was tired of fighting the good fight all alone and woefully unarmed. She thought about calling him just to visit. She went for a swim instead. She had to keep herself in the pool and the hot tub because the pull to talk to him was getting stronger than she could bear.

And then her phone rang.

She jumped out of the pool, grabbed a towel, and ran into the house to grab the phone. She tried to always answer her phone in case her kids needed her. It was a number she didn't recognize. She hesitated and thought if it was important, they would leave a message. But what if one of the kids lost their phone and needed a ride home? She grabbed the phone before voicemail did and answered. And it was him on the other end of the line.

"Hello? Please don't hang up!" He plead. And he sounded so sincere, so hurt, lonely. Victimized, even. She felt compelled to hear him out. He explained that he was at such and such hotel in this other town and they had an excellent restaurant up on the top floor with a beautiful view. He asked her to meet him there as he needed to talk with her.

And she had a question or two for him that she wanted to gauge his reaction to.

Back in the hot, oily bubble bath she went! Only this time she was in her own bath. No negative person between her and her bathroom. She made herself a rather stiff drink and then doctored up her bathtub. She wanted to look, feel, and smell ravishing. She wanted to make him want her. And then she thought about the rumors. But nothing had been proven. There were still no leads anywhere. The police had stopped by a couple of times, asking questions, and hoping to talk with her husband, but she had to tell them he didn't live there for now, that she wasn't certain just where he was. He calls her when he gets settled and leaves a contact number. But he works at the bank each day. Did they try to find him there? And the police informed her that he had taken a leave of absence to deal with the issues that had generated right in his own home.

And now she had more questions. Where was he staying? How long was he staying? Was he going to return to work? What were his plans for their marriage? They hadn't been married very long. It should be a simple matter.

She shook her head to get rid of all the negative spider webs setting up shop in her brain. It doesn't have to be a bad thing, going to meet him. She wanted to know if the rumors were true. Did he kidnap that girl right from their front room? But how did he do it because nobody woke up! No screaming, no kicking, no fighting, nothing broken, missing or in disarray. He couldn't have been the one. She had to have gone outside for a bit. Maybe even taken a swim. Maybe skinny dipped and someone saw her and crossed the line.

Deal with the here and now, Girl! She looked at herself in the full-length mirror and appreciated what she saw. All those laps in the pool. The aquacise exercises she did in the pool, sometimes with resistance weights. It pays off. She was still a very attractive woman, even coming up on 50 years old.

She smelled fantastic from her bath, but she also lightly spritzed on some perfume she had spoiled herself with. It was in a beautiful tiny little cut crystal atomizer. The bottle itself was beautiful but the scent it held was charismatic. It was what she wanted to portray. Maybe he would be so enthralled with all the work she put into her appearance tonight that he would slip and tell her the truth. Or maybe she would be able to help him open up enough so that she could see for herself he was innocent.

My gawd. How will this play out tonight? As a precaution, she called a friend and told her where she would be tonight, just in case. She hung up the phone after sharing her info and shivered.

Hoping it was the weather, she grabbed a pretty little shawl from the closet and wrapped herself in it. She rubbed her arms and warmed up a bit. As she opened the door and stepped out, she realized it was too warm and muggy for a shawl. She stepped back in the doorway and tossed the shawl across an entrance table, grabbed her keys and walked out the door.

He was staying a couple of towns away. It would take about 45 minutes to get there, but it was a really beautiful drive. She wasn't going to mind this at all. A warm evening drive, excellent dinner, adult conversation and then back home for a swim, a nightcap and bed, all by herself. Maybe even with some answers that fit. Maybe some answers for the police to sift through.

The police. They had been as respectful as they possibly could but still didn't seem to find any answers. Most of them knew her and her family before the second husband came along. They knew her to be the loving, honest, full of integrity lady she was, so they treated her gingerly but still wished to ask some pretty harsh questions about her new husband.

As she considered some of the questions the police had asked her, she wondered where they may be in the investigation. Had they located him? Did they know where he was? How sure were they that he was a suspect? Weren't there other registered offenders they could chose from? Maybe someone from the nearby larger cities? They could easily drive over to quiet, unsuspecting Anywhereville

America, rob it of its innocence and then head back to the big city to hide out with the rest of the gutter rats. Evil has no boundaries. But, why were they focusing on her husband? Because he was an unknown commodity? Nobody knew much about him so let's hang the new guy, right?

But what if? What if she finds out that he has a criminal record? Even if just for a white-collar crime, it would still be a violation of rules. A stepping over of boundaries. Her thinking completely flipped over, and she began wondering how she could prove to the police he was innocent. What if she kept in contact with him and reported their conversations and whereabouts back to the police? Eventually they would find the guy and it wouldn't be her guy. Because she might be with him and she would know without a doubt, that he was indeed the gentle, loving man she fell in love with. She considered calling the police and running the idea past them. She was told they don't usually ask civilians to put themselves in harms way, but they would love some sort of break in the case. Even if she did prove it wasn't him, they could stop trying to run that trail because she would have proof. They could focus on something else.

As she was reaching for the phone, she realized she needed to get going or she would be very late. Those police could keep you in their grips for hours! Days. Years. She would gauge tonight and see how she felt and then deal with the police tomorrow.

Geeze. How did she get here? How did this happen? Did she fall asleep these past few years? She had tried to be so careful, looking for red flags, bells and whistles. But she didn't see them. Maybe she didn't want to. It felt so nice to have a handsome man pay attention to her. And her husband was buried, so…

She drove with her window down and enjoyed it all. She pulled into the hotel parking lot and parked under the lights, close to the door where it will be well lit and well populated. Where she would be safe. She hopped out of her car and walked into the hotel lobby. This was one of her favorite hotels, but she never could justify coming here just for dinner. Or a night. She just lived down the road. So now was a great time for her to satisfy her curiosity about this lovely and regal place. When she walked in, a young maître d' appeared from virtually nowhere and asked if she was here to see her husband and rattled off his name. He escorted her to his table and explained that it may be a bit of a wait, but not much since it was still relatively early. He asked if she wanted the barkeep to play some music so they could dance.

Déjà vu. Was that his MO? Did he do this apparently very successful routine with every potential woman? It worked once. It was almost working a 2nd time, but still, there were questions that she didn't really want answers to. But she had to. For herself, her kids, her community.

A few people whispered behind their hands when they saw them together. It had been the first time in a long time, and she didn't care what they thought. She declined the dance and requested a drink. Make it a double! She always wanted to say that, and this time seemed perfectly fitting. Do you mind if we just talk right now?

And so, he began. He answered questions she didn't ask. He shored up his alibis. Why did he bring up alibis? He said it had been so difficult for him because he missed her and the kids so much. He missed her cooking, her laughter, the way she responded to him late at night. She felt her heart melting and had to pull herself back from the brink so many times. He was so smooth; seemed so genuine and sincere. And she was so lonely. Stressed. Depressed. Emotionally and physically drained and she needed someone to hold her, whisper in her ear that it will be ok. Someone who would be there for her, console her, build her up and get her back in the fight. She wanted that so badly. And then she realized it was he that was at the center of this mess! How could she possibly seek comfort from someone who has destroyed so many lives? Or did he? She definitely needed to get out in the woods, take the kids camping and have a very long talk with God. She was so confused. How could she be in this situation if all God wanted was for her to be happy? This feeling is not happy! She could feel her eyes stinging as they got ready to downpour! But she couldn't. She had to be strong, stoic, an investigator! Straighten the spine, chest out, suck in air and get your armor on. It's time for some truth telling! She giggled at the thought of her in armor. But then, maybe it wasn't so far-fetched. Women have become warriors. We've had to armor ourselves to fight for, fend for and protect our little ones. Especially when the male leaves us and we have to fight this all alone. A woman naturally grows her armor. And then she goes to work.

They shared another completely memorable meal together and then after dinner drinks and even shared a dessert. They were really enjoying their time together, even if every so often she saw someone staring at them. Pointing and talking about them. He suggested they go upstairs to his room for more privacy. He stopped at the bar and ordered more drinks and a couple of bottles of very nice wine. They had the bar in the room, but he'd gone through most of it, and they didn't carry her favorite wine in the rooms usually.

They stood close together in the elevator, each feeling a bit nervous and scared with each other. Things could go smoothly, or things could go south very quickly. He was hoping for smoothly. She was a logical person, a rational, thinking woman who didn't usually react with yelling and screaming. She believed that people in polite society should be reasonable enough to reach a compromise without anger, surely without resorting to fighting. So, he hoped she would continue to hear him out.

He didn't try to blame anyone else. He didn't claim to have been framed. He didn't take responsibility for the girl's disappearance at all. It was as if he was trying to distance himself from what was happening. He was, however, trying desperately to plant the tiniest seed of doubt in her mind. He may need her on the witness stand. Even he suggested the girl had gone for a walk, headed back to her home to get something, gone outside for a bit and was abducted then.

And she wanted to believe him so badly. She wanted something concrete to shove in the faces of the townsfolk and prove them wrong. Even though he offered a bit of doubt, there were still questions. What about the girl in the town he was originally staying in? Why did he leave? When did he leave? Before or after the 2nd girl was abducted? What was his timeframe? What is his game? Who da fuk is he?

He said he left because of the 2nd girl. He had already been deemed guilty without the benefit of trial and jury, so he hightailed it out of the town where girl #2 was kidnapped.

Makes perfect sense, right? Maybe too perfect. Don't innocent people take a stand, stay in place to clear their names? They didn't run like a coward and hide until people forgot about it. And he was definitely hiding.

She excused herself to go freshen up in the Ladies room. She passed the newspaper vendor as she did so and she stopped dead in her tracks at the headline of the local newspaper, It was in just the local paper, with medium sized fonts declaring that a 3rd teenage girl had gone missing in their town. It was legally in a different state, a different jurisdiction, but still, it should be screaming all over the national and outlying newspapers! This was a big deal. Teenaged girls were going missing and was anyone connecting the dots? She grabbed the newspaper and placed it firmly in her bag. She would take it to the local police and ask them why they hadn't considered these 3 cases related? Why aren't they alerting this area that there is a stalker out there taking our baby girls before they graduate high school. Before they walk down the aisle and become a Mama.

And why was it happening in the same town as her husband? Again. For the 3rd time. What an amazing coincidence. And all he had to offer was smoke and mirrors. She really wanted to believe him, to bring him back home, start all over. Be a family again. But then she remembered it didn't pan out that way last time. That was her fantasy, and it probably would never become a reality.

Still, he was here, right in front of her. Living, breathing, smelling too good manliness! She really had to hold herself back. He was a very good lover. Maybe from so much practice? She was just flip flopping back and forth. For each positive, she would bring up a negative. She was trying so hard to keep it balanced. She needed to seem logical, reasonable, and rational when she talked with the police. She also couldn't come off as a bitter, spiteful soon to be ex-wife. She would take the newspaper article and her gut feelings and sit down with the police and let them know what she's learned.

They sat apart from each other. More like they were squaring off than an estranged couple trying to get back together. The alcohol, as delightful as it was, didn't help diminish the stress this time. She kept waiting for him to break and tell her the truth. He kept planting seeds of doubt in her mind. She decided she had to go. She thanked him for dinner and drinks, for the talk and that she would like to discuss their marriage at some point. He offered to talk with her now, but she was too knotted up to talk any longer. She suddenly felt fear. She was having trouble breathing and felt like a panic attack was going to hit her full force at any time. She had to leave. He begged her to stay, and she thought about it briefly. Just crawl into that big, luxurious bed and let him make passionate, desperate love to her. Nobody would know. But she would. She would feel guilty sleeping with a man who may have abducted 3 young girls. She would actually have to pull up stakes and move.

Without warning, a chair went flying across the room! It nearly hit the sliding glass doors leading to the balcony! She looked back at him, mouth agape, and tried to will herself to breathe!

"Where in the hell did that come from?" she could only describe it as a screech. She had never witnessed this level of anger or violence. Maybe she hadn't witnessed any type of violence. She knew people got mad, but it seemed her family could deal with issues without violence. This was totally from left field and her mind was reeling trying to make sense of this.

"I'm just so angry that I'm being blamed for this and you believe it!"

"Whoa! I don't honestly know what to believe! If I had felt you were some sort of serial killer, do you think I'd be alone in this hotel room with you?" And then she scared herself. She didn't mean to bring it to his attention that they were alone. No witnesses. Just like her husband's accident. And who had called it in? It had always remained an anonymous good Samaritan that just happened to drive by. That just happened to be in this very hotel room with her. And with no witnesses. Rather than panic, she knew she had to stay calm. Be the force that brings this to an acceptable ending. Stay relaxed. Calm him down.

"You think I'm an animal like everyone else does! I know it!" he growled at her. And there it was. She saw it with her own eyes. His entire face changed into someone she couldn't recognize. His face scrunched up, lines, wrinkles, folds, shadows, valleys, all in this one face, all at once. He spewed his anger at her. His breath was hot, spiteful, nasty. But his eyes! They were pure black! Not the beautiful baby blue he usually showed the world. My gawd, does he wear contacts? Blue contacts? What color is his hair naturally? Who is this person?? And why is she alone with him. No witnesses. She could see he was going to escalate. His breathing became heavier. He looked like he really wanted to hit something, or someone. He began sweating and even his voice became darker, deeper. She was scared beyond anything she'd ever felt before, but she also knew he could most likely spiral out of control and the outcome would not be ideal.

She could see it now. She steeled herself and took a step closer to him. She looked lovingly into his face, as difficult as it was, and said softly, "I believe you and I need you to help me prove your innocence. That's why I'm here love, to help bring you back home to me where you belong."

He glared down at her, inhaled deeply, and raised his right arm high in the air.

"NO!!! You don't love me! Nobody does! I am unlovable and I'm going to make everybody pay!" And he brought his arm down, ready to hit her with the back of his hand as hard as he could. He wanted to hit her so hard, his entire childhood would have been wiped out. The beatings he witnessed. The beatings he endured. Being forced by his father to watch as he abused his puppy. The only one who loved him and was kind and gentle to him was that puppy. And his father knew it.

He wanted to hit her so hard, her head would snap, and blood would fly all over the room and he could finally walk alone again, without the demons that seemed to follow him around, taunting him. Just before his heavy fist landed in her face, he looked at her. Actually looked into her lovely face, her deep, caring eyes. Her gentle and generous soul and realized she could be the path to his salvation. He could see that she cared, and he began to wonder if he had finally turned himself into a man who was worthy of such a wonderful woman? Had he worked so hard trying to exorcise his father and his background, that he had finally succeeded? He really was a good man now. And he would begin following that path. And with her help.

He stopped, arm poised midair, and grabbed her, pulled her in tightly and broke down. He cried and wailed and held her so close she had to work for her air. But he wasn't doing it on purpose. He had broken. She was hoping now that he would finally sit back and take a deep breath, realize where he is, what he's done. And what's the next step?

She sat down hard on the lovely, luxurious, bouncy bed and had to take stock. What just happened here? What is going on? Who is this person I'm alone in a hotel room with? I know he's my husband, but who is he also? She had heard some of her friends complain that somewhere along the marriage line, their husbands had changed. They became secretive, uncaring, hiding things. Darkness around them. The ladies would say things like "I have no idea who I married!" Or "I don't recognize him anymore!" "He's a stranger to me."

One woman lamented that she was so tired of putting the house to bed by herself; finishing up dishes, getting things ready for the next day, checking doors and windows, making sure the animals are doing ok. And then she'd walk down the long hallway, all the while staring at the red and black checkered logger shirt and wondering who he was now. Why did he seem to hate her so much? She hadn't changed. They didn't have babies yet. She spoiled him rotten at every opportunity. Always had fresh baked cookies in the cookie jar. She stayed home and did everything she possibly could think of to make him happy. And it broke her heart to realize he would never love her again like he had the first couple of years. It wasn't just that the "newness" of the relationship had worn off, it was that he was just a player and he had found a new sandbox to explore. Apparently, she was still useful to him or he would have left her already. But he knew she loved him more than he had a right to be loved and he kinda enjoyed the feeling. From a large family of 9 siblings, to being basically an only child under her gentle and efficient hands.

But when the nasty women in town turned him down, he came home mad. It had nothing to do with her. He had an entire sex & personal life of his own and she wasn't invited. It seemed impossible that someone could be so deeply in love and then become a stranger. Weren't you supposed to grow together as one? The foundation of your family? Roots and wings, right?

But now she could see how things can change in the blink of an eye, literally. She saw how deeply wrong she was about this man. His many demons came flying out and he couldn't put them back in fast enough. She saw the real him and it was more than frightening. He really could become a monster! How horrible for those young girls to have to see this kind of ugly before they die. To see this level of rage, anger, hatred. Just plain ugly evil. It just isn't right.

She knew now that she would call the police when she got back home, and she would tell them that she will help them. She will help them stop her husband before another innocent life is lost.

The next thing she knew, she was in her car, windows down, night air swirling all around. The stars seemed especially bright and twinkly. She felt happy but she knew she shouldn't. For some reason, she felt like she had escaped a horrific situation. She had dodged a bullet so to speak. Maybe even literally.

She loved feeling free. She was going to take a swim when she got home and then visit the police station first thing tomorrow morning. Hopefully they wouldn't think she was a basket case. At the very least, she was hoping maybe she would garner enough information to believe her husband was innocent. Do they have any other leads? Do they have anyone in jail yet? Please let them say yes.

But then the image of the monster in the hotel room surfaced and she kept thinking now, that he can't possibly be innocent. But maybe.

Bright and early the next morning found her at the local police station. She knew most of them. Went to school with some. Went to the weddings of others. Even a funeral or two. She took fancy coffees and lots of donuts. She knew it was cliché, but she wanted to start off this conversation in a lighthearted, happy note. She was hoping to have her husband exonerated so she could bring him back home, get life back to normal. But she kept feeling this nagging at the back of her neck. A tension. A burning in her stomach at times.

And she knew she had to tell the police about last night. Her husband had mentioned leaving town now that she'd been seen with him. He couldn't be just some schmoe off the street because everyone knew him as her new husband. And everyone knew her. So, she knew that even if the police asked her where he was, she could honestly say she didn't know. But that was also what she wanted to offer the police.

She had made a list of pros and cons as to why or why not it could be her husband. She finished with stating she had dinner with him last night and found this tiny little newspaper article. When she asked why it wasn't public knowledge, or why the local or national newspapers weren't publishing it, she was told it would likely cause a public uproar and have people buying up all of the guns and knives in the shops. It would begin a feeling of paranoia that the police were not ready to handle. They preferred to keep it quiet until they had more leads. They didn't need a bunch of vigilantes shooting up innocent people! She left the newspaper article with the police, so her children didn't see it, grabbed a donut, and left the station.

So much to think about. She needed to sort the thoughts in her head and the feelings in her heart. She was devastated. But the police seemed to want to talk with her, keep the lines of communication open. They all knew her to be an honorable person. She didn't lie, cheat, or steal from anyone. She offered her services, her cooking and baby-sitting skills when needed. She was a good person. Although they were pretty sure she wouldn't have had anything to do with that child's disappearance, until now she hadn't made herself available to the police department unless they knocked on her door. So, they didn't know exactly how she felt about things or what she knew until now.

She felt another swim coming on. She was fortunate that her 1st husband's death took care of all of her bills. She was able to stay at home with the kids and not have to worry about a thing. She was so sad that that was how it happened. She thought of her first husband and how much she loved him. Where was he? Why did he leave her? Why didn't he come and rescue her? She missed him so much, she just hung her head and cried.

She must have cried herself to sleep because she woke up when the front door opened and a gaggle of teenagers came tumbling into the house, punching, laughing, tripping each other. Right to the kitchen and some went for the pool. One boy jumped in, clothes and all.

She was thrilled they were home and felt comfortable enough to bring their friends home. It was like old times, and she had really missed it. She wasn't sure when her home became so aridly controlled to almost the point of wasteland, but that didn't matter now. Her babies were here, they were safe and happy and healthy and that was all she needed right now.

Life goes on as it does, and the rumors died down. No other girls were taken that they knew of anyway. Tensions eased, windows and doors were left unlocked again. People were out and about and greeting each other. Her children all met their life's partner and were married. She had grandbabies now to keep her company. She kept in touch with her 2nd husband off and on. Somehow, a girl seemed to be missing in each town he resettled to. They talked about the chances of that happening, right?

Eventually the girl's disappearance became, unfortunately, a cold case. And every time he contacted her, she was confident he would already have been on the move again. Another town, another teen. The police lost interest because they lost jurisdiction. They submitted all of the information they could possibly provide but they had no new leads. But the baby girl was still gone. And there was still a small layer of sadness to this lovely little town, where crime never happened. And everyone knew everyone's parents, grandparents, aunts, uncles, cousins, neighbors.

She completely quit dating. It was just too scary, too dangerous. If she did go out, it was with someone she had known all her life. But she had these grandbabies to play with now. She loved being a GrandMa! They all possessed special talents and abilities, and they were all very bright children. Alert, aware, thoughtful. As they grew older, she developed wonderful relationships with each child. Some were artistic and creative. Some were serious and logical. Some were whimsical and funny! She loved each one equally. She also loved how easy being a GrandMa was! So much easier than being a single Mother, newly widowed, with 3 teenagers. She loved being a GrandMa.

They camped out in her front room. They camped out in the great outdoors. They camped out in their Mom's van, where we drained the battery singing karaoke and pissed their Mom off. They mostly chose helping professions. They became nurses, teachers, police officers. One of her beloved GrandChildren even became a lawyer! She loved the law and greatly enjoyed talking over cases with him. She especially loved the twists and turns of the cases, the saving grace of obscure law. Or sometimes it brought the death knell. He would give her a case such as felony assault or GTA and the verdict of guilty or innocent and make her figure out why. She loved to pick the case apart and see how closely she got to the jury's reasoning. They would discuss cases where the person seemed so sympathetically innocent and yet the jury held them guilty! Some that seemed just mean and cruel and with not an innocent bone in his body and they are deemed innocent. Of that crime, anyway. She loved trying to figure out why. He would bring over a random city's newspaper and discuss the cases inside. He would explain his strategy if he were the attorney on file for that case. He talked about cases where the guy was obviously guilty but jauntily exited the courtroom a free man.

One day her GrandSon came in and with an obvious hurt and pained tone to his voice asked why we hadn't ever discussed "my case". What do you mean, my case? I don't have a case. I've never even been to court. I haven't sued anyone, and nobody has sued me, thankfully.

You know, the case of your 2nd husband, the serial killer. And there it was! Put out before her without judgement. But the words, her husband and serial killer in the very same very short sentence. Her throat clutched and she couldn't breathe. She could see now that it had hurt him not to have discussed it earlier with him but seriously, she had spent so much time trying to forget that all happened, she didn't wish to dredge it all up again. She hadn't thought of all that for years and she preferred it that way. Her

2nd husband became history. A long-ago history. The girls' families tried to move on as best as they could. It was obvious some healed, some stayed right where they were, a prisoner in a time capsule, wrapped in sheer grief. She often cried for them late at night. But she hadn't even done that in a very long time.

She locked it away and threw away the key years ago. And now it was reopening thanks to her young lawyer GrandSon. He was bringing it out into the light of day to be aired into oblivion. She answered his questions as best she could remember. He brought her updates on her husband #2. True to form, he moved from one small town to another. He would move into a town, stay for a while, be noticed, date a little bit, maybe get married again and then a young girl would go missing and a few days later, so would he. Her GrandSon brought her newspaper clippings of similar crimes seemingly along a national path. One state, then another. Was it leading some place? Could you guess the next direction, the next town and maybe save a teenage girl unspeakable hurt, grief, possibly a violent death. What else could he be doing with them? He arrives and leaves each town by himself. And the girls never do come back home.

After several years of pain, hobbling around, eating Tylenol like they were candy and swimming and soaking in her pool and hot tub, she finally relented to getting her hip replaced. She was coming up on 70 but still lively, still vital. She was about to become a Great GrandMa and she wanted to be able to get around with this child too.

She made the arrangements with her doctor and the doctor made arrangements with the hospital. She met with the surgery crew and was put at ease by their expertise. The fact that they got along well and had obviously worked together for a long time made her even more comfortable. They would have no problem double checking each other's work. They would be grateful for the extra set of hands, ears and eyes and she would be in even better hands.

Her lawyer GrandSon had helped her get checked in, waited while they hooked up her IV and got her TV settled, got her a hot chocolate and something to nibble on before midnight, and sat with her for a little while. He brought in a newspaper from Florida this time. They were going to light up "Old Smokey", the Florida State electric chair! She would read that article after her GrandSon left. They discussed "her case" for a while and she was told that they had lost track of her 2nd husband yet again. He had a formula all worked out where he was gone and hidden from the law before they found the crime scene. He was beyond slippery. He was more like a phantom. You never knew where he might pop up. They discussed where he may have slithered off to this time, maybe which direction he might head, and then it was time for visitors to leave for the night. And she needed to get ready for her surgery tomorrow morning. She was so grateful it would be bright and early! She wanted it over with as quickly as possible so she could begin to heal and be the GreatGrandMa she wanted to be!

She rested for just a moment. She closed her eyes, willed herself to relax her tense muscles, and she began deep breathing. In with the good, out with the bad.

She felt rather than heard a presence in the room but when she opened her eyes, there was no one there. She couldn't help but shiver and grabbed the freshly heated blanket they draped over her legs and lap. She would rather not follow that line of thinking and make herself nuts, and what's to say it's not the meds making her freak out a little?

She fanned herself with the newspaper, not realizing how hot she had gotten so quickly.

She sat up in the bed, adjusted the pillows, poured herself a bit of water and sat back to read the newspaper her GrandSon had left for her. She didn't know anyone in Florida, so she was intrigued as to whom Old Smokey was going to get this time. Florida was a big time Good Ol' Boy system for years so they made a big deal out of lighting up Ol' Smokey. It usually made the national news. Probably as exciting as the missiles they fire into space heading for the moon in Cape Canaveral.

She took a sip of cold filtered water and sat back, opened the newspaper to the middle section and nearly passed out! It felt like someone had grabbed her by the throat, reached down and pulled her heart right out of her chest. There, on both sides of the middle pages of the newspaper, was the story of the man they were going to fry in the electric chair in the morning. It was the very same man that had tried to pick her up so many years ago when she had broken down on the side of the road. He was an old man now but had been caught in the act of abusing a young girl he had just stolen off the street. She was barely alive, but they rushed her to the hospital anyway where out of sheer will, she survived. She wanted to put the bastard in prison and that is what made her fight for her life so hard. So, they had witnesses and a surviving victim and they all ID'd that man. The man Ol' Smokey was gonna smoke. Apparently, he also was a serial killer.

About this time, her lawyer GrandSon got an incoming lead that his GrandMa's 2nd husband was in town! He grabbed his phone and ran to his car. He wanted to see his GrandMa in person and show her the message. He wanted to make sure she was OK. Something just didn't feel right. He drove as fast as he possibly could to get to the hospital. He had to warn her to watch out for him! Not that he would harm her, but why would he be here other than to tie up some loose ends? Did he consider her a loose end? She tried to be non-threatening, calm, relaxed around him so as to not piss him off and stir up his ire. She didn't want to be one of his targets. Why would he come back to hurt her at this late date?

As she looked up from the newspaper article, she saw a male nurse walk in with a syringe full of clear fluid. He was squirting just a bit of it out to make sure there was no air in the syringe.

"This will help you sleep the night before your surgery, young lady." Said the male nurse. He looked oddly familiar, and she felt a huge bit of tension in the back of her neck again. She got a text from her GrandSon telling her he was heading over and to be careful whom she allowed in her room.

And seriously, what could she do? She was in so much pain with her hip, there was no way to outrun them. She was full of pain meds as well, which might help her run, but would definitely cloud her judgement. She had no idea what to do so she hedged her bet by telling the nurse she needed to wait until her GrandSon came by to say goodnight. That it was a thing with them and that he was on his way. Maybe if this "nurse" knew this, he would leave and let her find a way out.

At least, she would have a logical, rational, educated soul to help her look at things clearly. She asked again to wait on the sleeping meds until her GrandSon arrived. They were going to have hot chocolate together the night before her surgery.

But still the "nurse" kept walking slowly towards her IV pole. Once he plunged it into the port, she was helpless. As she turned to yell for help, or look for her nurse's call button, which she couldn't find anywhere, she noticed there were nurses at the nurses' station across from her doorway and she yelled for them to help her! I'm not ready to go to sleep yet she yelled, and when they turned around, she knew, immediately, there would be no surgery in the morning. There would be no morning for her. They had all caught up with her somehow. They had burrowed into her life like a tick at various times and she had found a way to eliminate them, one by one. But now they were here, ambulatory and she was stuck in a hospital bed barely able to walk let alone run for her life.

She made out her odd childhood neighbor boy, all grown up. He was the one who lived around the corner. He was the one who wet his pants on the bus every day on the way home. Sometimes on the way to school too. He was the one who's Mama couldn't explain all of the dead animal bodies littered here and there around his yard. Sometimes a dead animal would be left on the porch of someone this kid didn't like or was mad at. Everyone knew not to ever hire him as a pet sitter. You'd come home to your pet's pelt gracing the back of your couch. He was the one who came to visit your 2nd husband and they would immediately leave the area together, lost in the fog of whatever was exciting them at the time. Did they share victims? Or did they just share their stories of what they did with the victims? Before she could explore that idea, she noticed the guy behind the desk. She remembered him from many years previously. One of the times she had snuck off to see her 2nd husband. She wanted so much to believe in the goodness of people. But this face had been taking up her husband's time when she arrived at yet another exquisite hotel. They were so engrossed in each other's words the maître d' had to clear his throat 3 times before they acknowledged us. And then the gentleman quickly jumped up, bowed slightly and put his hat in front of his face. But she remembered the face.

"No! Please don't do this! Please let me have a few moments with my GrandSon! He'll be here any moment!" and as she looked in the eyes of the male nurse with the syringe of liquid, she realized that it was her 2nd husband! He really was here! And as she's begging him, telling him she never said a thing to anyone, he begins plunging the syringe full of liquid into her IV port. Almost instantly she feels her eyelids getting heavy. So heavy that she won't be able to fight it for long. She just wants to sleep, to forget, for just a moment.

She is certain she hears him softly say, "No witnesses."

And as she is preparing to give up totally and give in to the twists, turns and atrocities of life, the slings and arrows that came her way that she can no longer dodge adeptly, her armor rusted into place many years ago. Because usually grandmas don't need so much armor anymore, she hears her GrandSon running down the hallway yelling for his GrandMa...

"Grandma, wait! Wait!! I'm here!"

As he slides along the slick hallway to his grandma's room, he realizes it's all empty. The hallway is empty of doctors or nurses milling about, saving lives by the minute. There are no visitors or orderlies. Nobody at the information desk or the nurse's station. It's totally quiet. He slides into his Grandma's room and looks at her. She's breathing softly. So quietly. At least he thinks she's breathing. As he stands there, feeling a little sheepish for being so dramatic, trying to take in the feeling of the room, the floor, he realizes things just don't seem quite right. He checks all of the whirring, buzzing, beeping noises and they seem to be working correctly. She is breathing for now but what was put in her IV? Would it actually be listed on her chart notes? He grabs them and begins reading. Everything seems to be in place and legitimate. He'd like to find a doctor to ask a few questions of about his GrandMa when she begins having trouble breathing. He grabs the oxygen mask to help her breathe and once she realizes it's her GrandSon, she pulls the mask off of her face and with genuine terror in her eyes, softly, so softly he can barely hear her, says,

"No witnesses!"

<div align="center">~~~End~~~</div>